Strength for the Journey

By

Francine A. Yates

Scripture quotations are taken from the King James Version of the Bible.

ISBN: 978-0-9778521-2-3 (paperback)

Published by Yates Publishing, LLC
P.O. Box 18982
Indianapolis, IN 46218
Printed in the United States of America

Fear thou not; for I am with thee: be not dismayed; for I am thy God: I will strengthen thee; yea, I will help thee; yea, I will uphold thee with the right hand of my righteousness.

Isaiah 41:10

Dedication

To Benjamin F. Yates, my beloved husband

My devoted children:
Donald L. Harrison Jr.
Patrice A. Fuller

My Granddaughter:
Amaya L. Greene

My Parents:
Leonard W & Ernestine Riggins Burnett

My brother & Sisters:
Frank Gossett; Terri Brooks; Valencia Rascoe;
Kathi Burnett;
Delia Burnett; Lezlie Burnett

Prayer Partners:
Minister Walter Rean Moore
Sister Josephine Charleston
Minister Doris Hill
Minister Carolyn Drane
Rev. Charles W. & Flossie Harris Sr., Pastor
Pleasant Union Missionary Baptist Church

Acknowledgments

First and foremost, I thank God for His grace and mercy. I also would like to thank Him for the gift of writing He has entrusted to me. I thank my confidant, and friend Etoria Wilson, for all she does to encourage me to keep writing. Also, Margie Shivers, who has been a God-sent in my life. I thank David Edy, my book cover designer. I thank Latasha Shobe, my niece, for reading, discussing, and believing in the story.

I am so thankful to all my friends who have stayed with me through all my up's and down.

To all the book clubs throughout the country and bookstores that have supported me, I thank you for adding *Strength for the Journey* to your book collections. And of course, to all my readers everywhere, thank you for supporting me!

Chapter One

Good morning Holy Spirit, I am here looking out my bay window, watching each drop of rain that falls. Lord, it is a cloudy, gray, and damp day. I sure hope the sun comes out and turn this into a beautiful sunny day. I've heard the old folk say if it rains on your wedding day, you will cry many of tears. I pray that is just an old wives tale. I love Jonathan and I know he loves me just as much.

My thoughts were interrupted by the ringing of the phone I couldn't help but to think *who is calling me so early and on my wedding day?*

"Good morning"

"Courtney, this is Ashley and I just wanted to see if you were up?"

"Girl, what are you talking about up? I've been up for two hours. I'm going to marry Jonathan Davenport today. Remember I'm going to be the first lady of Mount Goodwill Baptist Church."

"Yes, you are and you will be the envy of all of the young sisters in the church."

"I hope not, your brother's wife was murdered two years ago. He had two years to marry anyone in that church, but he chose me. I did a lot of praying before I said yes to him. I plan on being a good wife and a great mother to his three boys. Ashley if you don't mind, I better get off the phone, I have a lot to do before meeting you at the church. Thank you for being my best friend and flying in from New York to be with us on our special day."

Ashley and I have been the best of friends since we were in the ninth grade at North Central High School. The first thing I noticed about her was that she was tall and skinny like me. The next thing that caught my eye was her stylish clothing. Her jet black hair fell to her shoulders like satin. It was neatly combed and evenly cut. Most of us were wearing pants with short sleeve blouses, but she had on a long blue jean skirt and a sleeveless vest, with matching blue jeans shoes.

She introduced herself as Ashley Davenport and I told her that my name was Courtney Davis. We both noticed that since our last names started with a D we were in most of the same classes.

An embarrassing incident happened to me during our first week in gym. When it was time to take a shower, I was the only girl in the locker room walking around with a towel covering her entire body. I wasn't comfortable exposing myself like the other girls.

Heather Robertson thought she would draw attention to how I was walking around when she asked me why the large towel? I acted as if I didn't hear her and kept walking. She got loud and said we were all girls what did I have that was so precious that I needed to hide it. I didn't know much about her, just that she moved to Indianapolis from New York. The talk was that she had ties with the Mafia, which didn't mean a thing to me. All I wanted was for her to leave me alone to get my shower and dress for the next class. She was taller and bigger than me, and I guess I was going to be the person of the week for her to pick on.

I didn't want any problems with her, but when she walked up to me and snatched my towel. I wanted to knock her block off. But the next thing I knew Ashley hit her with a book-bag full of books.

Heather's legs went from under her and she hit the floor like a professional wrestler. Some of the girls started screaming like she was dead, while the ones who really didn't care for her, were laughing. All I remember is from that day on we didn't have any problems with Miss Heather and Ashley Davenport became my best friend.

Ashley would spend most weekends at my house, but I was never allowed to stay at her house. She had two older brothers and my family thought it would be best for her to stay with us. Ashley really enjoyed that because my little sister, Morgan, had her own room and my room had twin beds, but since Ashley was my company and Morgan was a year younger than me, we would let her stay with us most of the night in my room. When Ashley and I wanted to talk about boys we would tell Morgan that we wanted to call it a night, so she would have to go into her own room.

Morgan was short, petite and light-skinned like our mother. I was tall and brown-skinned like our father. Yet, you could tell that we were sisters because we both had our father's light brown eyes and long eyelashes.

Ashley liked to comb Morgan's hair because it was long and thick. She would talk about me because I was tender headed and all I wanted was to wear my hair pulled back in a ponytail. Ashley was the one who talked me into getting my hair cut in the front to wear bangs. She also taught me how to roll my ponytail into a neat ball on the back of my head.

Ashley's oldest brother's name was Derrick. He was three years older than her. He was the quiet one in the family. Her other brother, Jonathan, was two years older than Ashley. He would drive her to my house and pick her up when she was ready to go. I liked it when he drove her to my house because then I could see him. He had the most beautiful eyes. They were light gray, and that smile, it was so friendly. He would treat me like I was his little sister, but I could tell he thought I was cute. Often he would wink at me.

When I found out he was dating Violet Monroe I was so hurt. Even though she was his age, I still wanted to date him. I knew that he came from a good home and since his father was a preacher, I knew he would treat me like a lady. I hated Violet and wanted to end her relationship with Jonathan.

One day I mailed a letter to the Davenport's house for Jonathan. I told him that I was seeing someone else. I signed it Violet. Ashley told me that he was so angry he wouldn't talk to Violet. She said Violet was calling day and night trying to explain that she didn't write the letter, but Jonathan called off their relationship. To put my plans into further action, one day I rode home with Ashley to study, but what I wanted to do was talk to Jonathan.

He really didn't want me there. He told me to go to Ashley's room and study. That hurt, and after that incident all Jonathan did was study, work and talk about being a preacher. I never told a soul that I was the cause of his break up with Violet.

The phone started ringing again interrupting my thoughts.

"Hello"

"Courtney, this is Mother, do you want me to come over?"

"Mom, I have everything ready. I'll meet you at the church in two hours."

"All right, but before you hang up, let's have a short word of prayer. Dear Heavenly Father, thank you for this day. I thank you for blessing Courtney with a God-fearing man. I want you to please bless this marriage and most of all, help the boys to love her. Amen."

"Thanks, Mom, see you at the church."

Mom got that right! Those boys are something else. David is nine and he loves me. Dwayne is eleven and he treats me nice as long as his older brother, John, is not around. Fourteen year old, John's action toward me is as if I'm trying to take his mother's place. I've assured him in previous conversations that I would like to be his friend and his stepmother.

I know out of this marriage, John will be the one that keeps me on my knees praying and constantly asking God to give me strength for this journey.

I was about to gather my things to go to the church when there was a knock on my front door. Most of my friends use my side door, so I figured that this must be a wedding gift being delivered.

As I walked towards the door, there was another knock. This time a little louder, so I shouted "Who is it?"

A loud voice came from the other side of the door

"This is Granny, so open the door."

I opened the door. Granny was standing there with a serious look on her face. I said, "Granny, what are you doing here?"

She rushed pass me and said, "Let me take a seat. We need to talk. I want you to know that you are my granddaughter and I want you to be happy, but I don't think you should be marrying that preacher. His wife has only been dead two years and look at him, looking for someone to take care of those boys of his. I got one question to ask you. Why did you come back here when you were doing so well in Chicago?"

"Granny, this is my wedding day. Why are you coming here starting some mess? Jonathan loves me and I love him."

"You still didn't answer my question. I said why did you come back when life was so good for you in Chicago? What ever happen to that young man you were dating? You know Carl, Curtis, Calvin, what ever his name was?"

"Granny we don't have the time for me to go into all of that, I have a wedding to attend. And by the way his name was Curtis Wellington."

"Courtney, all I know is that he used to come home with you on holidays and he could eat like there was no tomorrow. Where is he anyway? And when Deborah died, we saw you here almost every other weekend. I guess you came here to comfort Jonathan. You better be true to yourself, by taking a long look at what you are about to get yourself into.

You are marrying a preacher that could have asked anyone in his church to marry him. Some would have said yes and some no, but you go on and take on this great responsibility. I heard that oldest boy don't like you. What makes you think he is going to fall in love with you after you marry his father? All I can say is you'd better pray now before it's too late."

"Granny thanks for your advice. I know God will bless this marriage and in due time the boys will learn to love me as their stepmother. I know you're just looking out for me, but I'm grown and can handle this."

"Somebody better look out for you. Your parents ain't saying nothing just letting you destroy your life, just so they can say you finally got married and just maybe you will give them a grandchild or two."

After Granny said how she felt, she got up and made her way to the door. I kissed her and she went on her merry way. I couldn't close that door fast enough. What in the world has gotten into my granny? She has visited our church and each time Jonathan and the boys have treated her with kindness and respect. I bet some of those old biddies at church have been gossiping about the pastor and how John feels about me.

Granny has a few friends that are charter members at our church and they probably are spying and telling her all the news. Mother Essie sits on the front pew, she and Granny has been friends all my life, but I don't see her saying anything, she is quiet and has a loving personality. Maybe it is that rolling eyes, flowery dress wearing Mrs. Jessup, she keeps up so much trouble in the church. I think she hates everyone when she doesn't get her way.

I remember when I joined the church. She rolled those big eyes at me. She then looked me up and down as if she wanted to say something about me wearing pants in the church. I just looked in another direction and vowed to stay out of her path.

After I completed my four weeks of new membership class I was supposed to be assigned to her Sunday school class, but I declined. I went to the young-adult class.

One Sunday morning, she came rushing up to me, she wanted to know why wasn't I in her class? She said I surely was old enough to be in her class. I told her I wanted to be in the young- adult class for a while. I would eventually graduate to her class. That didn't quite sit too well with her because in our church meeting, which happened to be the very next month she brought it to the church. She stood in the middle of the aisle as if she was showing off her new pink flowery dress, with her white slip dipping a little under the dress. She usually has on blue, green, or purple. Except for first Sunday when she wears her white suit.

She said why don't we combine all the adult women in one class? Never mind the age since everyone isn't obeying the rules. She didn't call out my name, but after giving her statement she looked over at me and nodded her head. Pastor Davenport told her he would take her suggestion into advisement and went on with the meeting.

I think she has hated me every since. I know when she found out that we were getting married she stopped speaking to me. This was good for me, because every time I would try and set up a new program I would have to hear from her, "Deborah wouldn't have done it like that?" Several times I wanted to tell her Deborah was dead and I will soon be the first lady and I demand respect. I knew that she would never accept me since Ashley shared with me that she was Deborah's God mother. But, as I look back I can see how God has kept me even back then. It is simply amazing to see how the Lord has brought me through many obstacles so that He could prepare me for the challenges that were to come.

Chapter Two

My Granny's words kept ringing in my ears. Why did I move back here from Chicago?

She had the nerve to say Curtis' name. He and I broke up six months before Deborah died. Curtis was a user. He had the nerve to quit his job and got angry when I refused to pay his rent. He asked if he could move in with me until he found a job. I told him my parents didn't raise me to be a fool. So, he would call my home, office and bugged my friends to try and get back into a relationship with me. I told him to forget he ever met me. I got so tired of his advances that I changed my home telephone number. At work I asked the receptionist not to put his calls through. Finally, he got the message and stopped harassing me.

Six months later Ashley called to tell me that Jonathan's wife, Deborah, was out delivering blankets to the homeless, when one of the men attacked her. She never regained consciousness. I always liked the way Deborah would treat Ashley and me when we were in her company. She had a great personality and just loved everyone. We had something in common. Both our families originally came from Augusta, Georgia. She used to say we looked a little alike and just might be related.

She and Jonathan started dating in their last year of high school. They were so well liked that they were crowned king and queen at the senior prom. Jonathan eventually got the nerve to ask her to marry him. She wanted to attend Ivy Tech State College, and land a job at the *Indianapolis Star Newspaper.* Jonathan got hired at the Ford plant. He worked the second shift and took classes in the day. His plan was to become a minister and he wasn't about to let anyone stand in his way.

I think Ashley knew that I had a crush on her brother because she would often pick me up on her way to their house. When we would get there I would find myself searching for Jonathan. I was really happy for Deborah, but at the same time wanted it to be me.

Deborah's parents moved to Anderson, Indiana after she graduated from high school. She would take trips there often to visit them. I remember once when Ashley and I were in college. It was summer break; we had no plans other than coming home to visit our parents. Jonathan was preaching in Anderson and most of his family was going there to support him. Ashley asked me to join them. I was so happy.

We drove up early that Sunday morning. Jonathan was so happy to see his family and me too. I wasn't dating anyone in college, I just wanted to be near him, but he always treated me like I was his second sister. However, I couldn't fool my mother. She could see the gleam and sparkle in my eyes meant only for him.

Deborah got pregnant in their first year of marriage. This made Jonathan's parents very happy. All his mother talked about was being a granny for the first time. Of course, the first baby was a boy. Three years later she gave birth to their second son, and two years later, David was born. Oh how Deborah wanted a girl. She used to say if it was God's will, she would have a daughter.

It brings tears to my eyes thinking about the dream that never came true for Deborah. She was a great first lady to Mount Goodwill Baptist Church. I hate it that her life was cut so short, when it seemed as if she had it all but God knows best. After her death, he placed me in Jonathan's life and I plan to be the very best wife he could ever ask for.

However, I'm going to have to stand my ground with the boys and with some of those members at the church. I feel I shouldn't have to walk in Deborah's shoes. She did her part while on earth, now it is my time to shine.

There was another knock on the door. I wondered who in the world was outside making all of that noise?

"Courtney, aren't you going to let me in?"

I rushed to open the door and there stood my good friend Brittany Reynolds. "Brittany, come on in. Why didn't you call before coming here? You know I have boxes everywhere and I still have to be to the church in a few hours."

"Why am I here? I came in my brother's pickup truck to help you haul some of the boxes to your new home."

"Brittany, these boxes are going into storage, my parents will be taking them for me. I think you came over to see the dress."

"Okay, you got me, I do want to see the dress and to see if you've made up your mind to call this thing off. You know that older boy, John, is crazy. I know because I teach at his school. Since his mother died he has become a stone nut."

"Do you mind if we hold this conversation after my honeymoon? I promise you can come to the house and we can share stories over coffee."

"You must be crazy! I don't drink coffee and especially since it is this hot outside. I'm a Pepsi lady all the way."

"Girl, you have been my friend since college, so I can tell you how I feel. See you at the church and don't let the door hit you on the way out!"

"Now don't take that attitude with me, just because your soon to be son, is crazy and has a nasty attitude. The only reason he's not kicked out of school is because he's a preacher's son and his mother was murdered."

"Thanks Brittany for the information, but I'm aware that the child is troubled, but I plan to work on his attitude towards me when I return from my honeymoon."

"Courtney, that boy is crazy and is in need of professional help. You better watch your back, and do much praying."

"Enough! I've got to get ready to leave."

"Hey, you forgot to show me the dress."

"You can see it at the church when I walk down the aisle on my father's arm."

She didn't say another word. She just opened the door and walked toward her parked car. I wanted to say something, but I just closed the door and shouted "Lord, What next?"

Chapter Three

Who's knocking on my door again? I'm never going to get to church. "Who is it?"

"Courtney, this is Barbara, Barbara Hall"

"Barbara, come in. What are you doing on this side of town?"

"I was coming from the church and I turned and saw several police cars near Pastor's house. What's going on?"

"I haven't heard from Jonathan today."

"You better call him, like I said I saw police cars all up and down his street."

I rushed to the phone. With shaking fingers I dialed his number. I waited and waited no answer. I looked at Barbara who was biting her finger nails and acting nervous.

"Let me call the church, he might be there."

I dialed the church and waited, finally I got an answer.

"Mount Goodwill Baptist Church, Darlene Brown is speaking."

"Darlene, this is Courtney"

Darlene has been Jonathan's secretary for the last ten years. Ashley said she has been one dedicated secretary to Jonathan and the church.

"Is Jonathan there?"

"You haven't heard?"

"Heard what?"

"Jonathan is at the hospital. John was over to somebody's house. They were playing with a gun and he got shot."

"What? Which hospital did they take him to? Is he all right? My God, Darlene is he alive?"

"Calm down Courtney, he only got shot in the foot. The other boy is in surgery."

"What other boy? Please don't tell me it is Pastor's other son?"

"No, the boy is John's age. They're at Wishard Hospital. You better hurry over to be with Pastor."

"Thanks for the information. I will see you later."

"Come on Barbara please let's rush to Wishard to see if we can find Jonathan and John."

Barbara was passing cars and running yellow lights making it to the hospital. Before I knew it, she was pulling to the front door of the emergency room. I got out and ran in looking for Jonathan.

A nurse was sitting behind the desk. She looked up and asked if she could help me. I told her I was looking for John Davenport. She looked on the computer screen and said he was released.

Just as she said that, Barbara was coming down the hall looking for me. I wanted to shout because his wound isn't that serious.

Just as Barbara and I were about to exit the emergency room a short lady with blond and brown hair came up to us. She had puffed red eyes, where she had been crying.

"I heard you ask about John Davenport, are you related

to him?"

"No, well yes, his father and I are getting married today, and who are you?"

"My name is Iris Blake, the accident happened at my house while I was at the store getting breakfast for the boys. When I left I thought they were all asleep. I am so sorry it's my fault. You see my husband does a lot of hunting and he usually keeps his guns locked in a case, but I guess this time he forgot to put one up. My son's name is Willie and he was shot along with John. The story I got out of the boys is that Willie was showing John and his other friend, Adam, how to handle a gun. When they started wrestling around with it, John was shot in the foot. The bullet glazed his big toe. He got a few stitches, but Willie got it in the arm. He lost a lot of blood and he's in surgery now, this is why I am still waiting out here. The doctor said it wasn't too serious, Thank God, Adam ran out, so nothing happened to him. I'm so sorry this happened on your wedding day."

"You have nothing to be sorry about. This was an accident and I'm happy that it wasn't more serious, than it could have been. I will keep Willie in my prayers, but in the meantime I need to find Jonathan and John."

"I understand, and thank you for your prayers. Good luck with your wedding today."

"Thanks"

I looked in my purse for my cell phone to call Jonathan, but it wasn't in there. Barbara said she didn't have a phone. I asked her to take me to his house. When we arrived, Jonathan was sitting on the porch with a worried look on his face.

I rushed to his waiting arms as he held me tight. I

whispered in his ear. I'm so happy John is all right."

Jonathan said, "He'll live, but he has messed up our wedding day completely. I'm happy that no one was killed, but I'm angry. I didn't want him to go to the sleep over, but he kept insisting that he would be home in time for the wedding, so I let him go. I should have said no and this wouldn't have happened."

Barbara said, "Look I'm going home and let you two talk things out. I'll see you at the church in a few hours."

"Barbara, I can't thank you enough for driving me around. Jonathan will see that I get back home. I will see you at the church."

I took his hand, placed it in mine. I looked him straight into his eyes and said, "Jonathan maybe we should call this wedding off. Maybe we should give John a little while longer to get his self together."

Jonathan snatched his hand out of mine and said, "Courtney, are you crazy! I refuse to allow John to mess up our wedding. He's been a problem since Deborah died. I just can't seem to get through to him. We have prayed, talked and I even sent him to counseling, but nothing seems to work. I want you to be my wife and the boys need you. Please don't call it off."

"Jonathan, if you think we can be a family, I'm willing to give it a try. Lord knows I have always loved you. Now get me your telephone so I can call a cab to take me home, you go inside and be with John."

"My mother is in there, she is probably looking out the living room window listening at what we are talking about. I will go in and tell her that the wedding is on and I will be right back. I need to take you home."

"I sure would like to go inside and have a little talk with John."

"No, I don't think that's a good idea. Besides, the pain medicine probably has him asleep."

I said okay and waited for Jonathan to go inside to talk with his mother. When he returned, we walked to the car. Just as I was about to get in the car, I noticed the curtain moving. I took another look and it was John looking out with a sad expression on his face.

Chapter Four

When I arrived at home I was surprise at the number of messages on my answering machine. I listened and decided to return only one call, that would be to my sister, Morgan. She would then relay the message to our parents. By now they should have heard about John and I wanted them to know that the wedding is still on. Morgan and I have always been close. She is the one that has always been quiet spoken and easy to get alone with. Even though I am the oldest I can talk to her about anything.

Her favorite words are "Trust God. While we are trying to figure it out, God has already worked it out." I smiled as I dialed her telephone number.

"Hello Morgan, before you say anything I want you to know that John is all right and the wedding is on."

"When I first heard I called the church and Darlene said it wasn't serious, so I called you to have a word of prayer. When I didn't reach you Christopher and I prayed for John."

Morgan met Christopher Hamilton in her last year at Purdue University. My parents love him. He's well-mannered and he loves her to death. They are getting married in a few months.

"Morgan, please call our parents and tell them I will see them at the church."

"Okay, I will see you later."

Hanging up the telephone, I walked pass the mirror and took a good look at myself. In a few hours I would no longer be Courtney Davis, but Courtney Davenport. I had gotten the man of my dreams and I refuse to let people like Mrs. Jessup or even his son John mess up my life.

After putting my suitcase in the car, I got my wedding dress, pulled the door to my apartment close and walked to my car. With a big smile on my face and my shoulders back, I strutted like a run way model. "Look out world here I come"

When I arrived at the church, I was happy that the entire wedding party was waiting. Cynthia got in touch with them all to meet two hours early, so we could rehearse, get dressed and have a word of prayer. I looked for John, but he was the only one missing.

"Morgan, where is John?"

"He is sitting upstairs, but you know he can't usher."

"I know, but the two younger boys will do a good job. I refuse to let anyone take my joy."

"Yes, say it like we were taught, this is the day that the Lord has made and I will rejoice and be glad in it."

"Morgan, give me a hug, you always comfort me. I hope and pray when you and Christopher get married I will be as helpful to you as you have been to me."

I looked around and saw Jonathan's two sons dressed in their black suits. They looked like two men. I felt a little sorry because I thought David was too young to be an usher, but due to John's accident, he will have to take his place.

"Come here David and Dwayne, you two look so handsome and I want to thank you for doing this for your father and me. This is the best gift I could have gotten. I want you to know that I love you and we are going to be a family."

Dwayne said, "Do you mean you will love John too?"

"Yes, I love John too"

Jonathan walked in and saw the three of us standing in the floor hugging. He had tears of joy in his eyes. He came over and put his arms around all three of us. I was thinking *thank you God for this moment.*

Cynthia made us all take a seat while she went over the plans. She told Jonathan, his best friend, Evan, and Jonathan's brother, Derrick to come from the side of the church along with Pastor Derrick Davenport Sr., Jonathan's father, since he was officiating the ceremony. Jonathan had to make a hard decision about having his older brother, Derrick, or his long time best friend, Evan, as his best man. Derrick stood up for him at his first wedding to Deborah, so he asked him how he felt about not being the best man this time. Derrick told him it is only fair that he ask Evan. As long as he was in the wedding party he was satisfied.

We all went upstairs to rehearse I couldn't help but notice the beauty of the church. I looked and saw all the white and pink roses; she had large pink bows on the first four seats. She then alternated with white bows on the other side of the church.

I looked over and saw that John was sitting on the last pew. He had such a sad look on his face. I decided after rehearsal I would go over and get him to join in when we have prayer. Cynthia made us practice one last time, she said for us to come to the back of the church for a word of prayer.

I walked over to John and said, "I'm sorry about your accident and would you like to join us in a word of prayer?"

He answered in a hateful tone he said, "why yes, I would love to join the circle, but don't you see my foot is bandaged."

I did what any normal mother would have done. I told everyone to let's get closer to John so he could be in the circle of prayer with us.

His grandfather led us in a word of prayer, and as he prayed I noticed John starting to hold my hand a little firmer. Just when I thought he was holding on because he cared, he tried to squeeze it. After prayer, he turned my hand loose and gave me a sly grin. I acted as if it didn't hurt. He shouted "you wish I was killed so you wouldn't have to deal with me."

I was shocked by the words that came out his mouth. I said "John, why would you say such a terrible thing? I'm marrying your father, but I love you boys as if you were my natural children."

He said "Well, you better get this straight! My mother's name was Deborah and she is the only mother I had! So don't be calling me your son. Like it or not, we are not a family! We were doing just fine until you came bursting into our life. We don't need you! Get away from me before I hurt you!"

I looked around and everyone in the wedding party was looking in my direction. The entire room went still. I could feel the blood rushing through my veins, but I swallowed my pain. I wasn't going to let John hurt me again; he has hurt me over and over again. Why should today be any different? Slowly I walked away and rushed to the ladies room.

I would hear Jonathan yelling at John, but I wasn't about to go back out there, not just now. I was too hurt to face everyone. Finally Morgan came to my rescue.

"Courtney, John is young and he is just letting the devil use him. You have been in church all your life and you should know Satan by now. Face him, go back out there and don't let John mess up your day. He has a problem and if I was you, when I got back from my honeymoon I would be sending this young man to some kind of boot camp for troubled youth. You have two other boys to raise. I'd refused to let him make me unhappy. If anyone was going to be unhappy, it would be him. Jonathan is so angry. He took his open hand and almost knocked John off that seat. John started yelling at his father that he was going to call the police."

"Morgan I'm very close to calling this thing off. I'm too hurt to walk down this aisle. This is getting out of hand. Please tell Jonathan to meet me in his office, we need to talk."

"Courtney, don't do anything stupid! You and Jonathan love each other and I just don't want to see you allowing John to take your happiness. That boy needs help."

"Go on Morgan, asked Jonathan to meet me in his office, and I mean right now!"

Chapter Five

I dried my tears, ducked out of the ladies room and headed straight to Jonathan's office. It was unlocked so I entered. Some of his pictures had been removed and recent ones of the boys and me were placed in the same spot.

I walked around Jonathan's mahogany desk. His opened Bible caught my attention. I looked to see what he was reading. It was turned out to the book of Ephesian 5. The twenty-fifth scripture was highlighted. *Husbands, love your wives, even as Christ also loved the church, and gave himself for it.*

I smiled to myself thinking he was reading this about loving me as Christ instructed him to do so. I then walked over and took a seat in one of his plush black leather chairs. I know that I love Jonathan and that I want to be his wife. I also know in my heart that something has got to be done about John. I kept thinking about what to say to him. Should I allow the Holy Spirit to do the talking for me?

Jonathan entered the office. He took a seat in the other chair next to me. I dried my tears, took a deep breath, and said "Jonathan, we definitely have a problem with John. He is doing everything in his power to mess up our wedding day, what do you suggest we do about him?"

"Courtney, after careful thinking, I decided the best thing for us all is for me to call Deborah's parents to come and get him while we are on our honeymoon. His grandmother said if it got to where I couldn't handle him, she would take him for a few weeks. I think today is the day for her to get him. She and her husband are okay with our wedding plans. They knew that I was a good husband to their daughter and they are happy for us. I will have one of the deacons to come and drive him home to pack. Then they can meet him at our house. The other two boys will continue with our original plans to stay with my parents."

"What if he doesn't want to go?"

"He has acted up for the last time, and I am losing my patience with him. Pastor or not, I'm ready to give him an old fashion beating."

"No Jonathan, just call his grandparents. Meanwhile, I'm going to get my makeup applied and dress for the wedding. I'll see you in a little while. I love you, and thanks."

Jonathan kissed me lightly on the lips. "I love you too and nothing is going to stop us from being together."

These were the most assuring words I had heard all day. I knew in my heart that I was stronger and was going to make it. I smiled and got up and headed for the door, while he walked around to the other side of his desk to make the call.

I felt as if a ton of bricks had just fallen off my chest. In a few minutes I would be Jonathan's wife, and soon John would be in the company of his grandparents. I knew that after the honeymoon I could talk Jonathan into letting him stay there until I get my things settled in our home. I smiled when I thought of that *our home.*

Everything went as planned, John was picked up by

his grandparents and I was ready to walk down the aisle with my father.

My father was handsome in his Michael Jordan athletic cut tuxedo. I was five feet nine inches, with heels. I didn't want to step on my long cathedral-length train. I looked up at my father. He was standing six foot two inches all smiles with his chest stuck out. He was proud and happy for me.

He told me that the only thing that was missing now was having a little granddaughter to bounce on his knee. I smiled and told him that hopefully that would be the next big venture in this marriage. We both laughed, Cynthia tapped on the door, so we could get in our position.

Cynthia opened the doors. My father looked down at me and said, "God bless you Courtney."

We headed down the aisle. All eyes were on us. The church was packed from the first pew to the last one. I smiled and the tears of joy filled my eyes. Jonathan was smiling at me. I smiled back, knowing that I finally got the love of my life. God knows, I can make it in this marriage.

Jonathan repeated his vows loud and clear, but I got choked up. I took a deep breath to gain my composure, while holding his hands tightly I said them loud and clear, so that everyone would know how much I loved this man.

I slipped his wedding band on his finger and he smiled. He slipped the two-carat white diamond ring on my finger and the sparkle of the diamond seemed as if it lit up the room. Pastor Davenport Sr. had to put a little humor in the ceremony because he made a comment on how large the diamond was. I could hear the congregation laughing. I was still a little nervous until I heard the minister say the groom could kiss his bride. Jonathan pulled my veil up and kissed me. Pastor Davenport Sr. then presented Mr. and Mrs. Jonathan Davenport to the invited guest. The entire church stood and clapped. My sister ran up to me and said, "See God has worked it out. You make a beautiful bride and I know you will be happy." I thanked her.

The photographer took plenty of pictures. The only let down was that there would not be any with John on them. Cynthia asked for us to form a line to greet our guest.

Finally, Jonathan and I were able to walk over to the room where the reception was to be held. As we entered, my eyes were drawn to the large four-tier, French vanilla-filled wedding cake. It was adorned with iced pink and white roses. Fresh pink and white rose pedals, adorned the table, accented with plenty of greenery. Jonathan and I had chosen an entrée of baked chicken, lamb chops, green beans, macaroni and cheese, tossed salad and dinner rolls.

After everyone was feed and the cake was cut and served, it was time for Evan to make a toast to us. Non-alcoholic Champagne was placed on each table.

We ended our day with a word of prayer from my father. Then most of the guest followed us outside to the waiting limo to throw confetti at us. Jonathan and I said our goodbyes and thanked them again for making our day a happy one.

Chapter Six

I woke up early with a praise song on my lips. I was so happy! I was alive to see another day and I was the wife of Jonathan.

I opened the curtains just enough to see what the day looked like. The sun was shinning bright. I knew it was going to be a good day.

I didn't want to wake Jonathan so I went into the bathroom to have a word of prayer with God. This is something that I do each morning. My prayer was simple.

"I will bless the Lord at all times and His praises shall continue to be in my mouth. I thank you God for this day and I thank you for this marriage and I know with you all things are possible."

There was a knock on the bathroom door. "Courtney are you using it or thinking that you made a mistake marrying me?"

I opened the door to a yawning man who was rubbing sleep from his eyes. Although he looked tired and sleepy, he was still as handsome as ever.

"Jonathan you are too crazy! I'm just brushing my teeth and praising God for this day. You may come in. I've got to gather my things. You did say we have a noon flight to make for our honeymoon?"

"Yes, and now I can tell you where we are going. We're

booked on a five day cruise to the Bahamas."

Squealing with excitement, I threw my arms around him and covered his face with butterfly kisses. "I knew you were taking me somewhere special. I have never been on a cruise before. My sister told me just in case you were planning one, to bring a copy of my birth certificate and passport. Did you let her in on the secret?"

"No, I didn't let anyone know where I was taking you. I wanted my wedding gift to you to be a surprise. I also booked a night stay on Paradise Island at this resort called Atlantis; it's where movie stars stay when they're on the island."

"Oh Jonathan, I can get used to this kind of treatment. I know we are going to have a wonderful time."

We both got dressed and headed downstairs to breakfast. We were staying downtown, at the Embassy Suite. It had a delicious breakfast bar.

As we dined, the boys crossed my mind. I wanted to call them to see how they were doing, but Jonathan suggested that, we wait until the honeymoon was over. They would really be ready to see us when we returned with our hands full of gifts for them.

After returning to our room, we packed and headed to the airport in the hotel limousine. As we drove along the busy highway, Jonathan pulled me close to him.

"So Mrs. Davenport how do you like being married?" He kissed me lightly on the lips.

"This is the best thing that has ever happened to me in life." I kissed him back. "I know that it isn't going to be easy with John, but I was willing to make this marriage and motherhood work."

He smiled. "I know you will."

The driver pulled just under the Delta sign and helped us out. While Jonathan handled the business of checking us in, I found myself watching him. He was such a handsome man, and so well dressed in his tan pants and short sleeved knit shirt. His black shoes were so highly polished that you could see your reflection in them. He looked good, but so was I in my basic black short sleeved Jones of New York pantsuit. I had on my matching, low heels dressed shoes.

As we walked down the concourse to our gate, we decided to go to the news stand to get a book or magazine, and who did we run into? None other than Mrs. Maxine Jessup.

"Pastor! Courtney! Of all the people in this world, I never expected to see you two. I just got back in town. I was out-of-state visiting my sister. She's been ill. How did the wedding turn out?"

I said hello and then stood there with a half smile on my face. I decided to let Jonathan do all the talking, since I knew she didn't like me anyway. He could have melted butter with his charm.

"Oh, Mrs. Jessup, it was very nice, standing room only. I'm so sorry you were unable to attend. How is your sister doing?"

"She's better. I'll probably go back before winter sets in. Where are you and Courtney going?"

"We are taking a cruise to the Bahamas."

"Oh that's nice. I remember you taking Deborah to one of those islands, either for her birthday or anniversary.

You two go on and have a good time. You know I'll hold down the fort until you return. By the way, Pastor, who's preaching while you're away?"

"Minister Holland, but I'll be back to preach next Sunday."

"Oh, really, I'm glad to hear that."

She prattled on and on about how much she would miss Jonathan's preaching while I stood there smarting at her comment about how my husband had taken his late wife to the islands previously. I wanted to walk away, but I knew that would be rude, and would only put gas on the fire. She would go back to the church and tell everyone who would listen about how rude I was to her. I stood there, with that half smile on my face, trying not to look bored to death.

Finally, she looked at her watch and said, "Well you two have a good honeymoon and I will see you next Sunday when you return."

Relieved, I said goodbye, but Jonathan gave her a big hug and kissed her on the cheek, then whispered, "God bless you Mrs. Jessup."

She walked away smiling like she had just been awarded queen for the day by the Mayor of Indianapolis.

Chapter Seven

The flight was smooth and on time. When we arrived in Orlando and exited the plane, we could feel the heat. The sun was definitely shining.

The airport was large and full of people. I didn't want to get separated from Jonathan, so I took his hand. After claiming our luggage, we noticed a man holding up a sign with our last name written on it. Jonathan informed him that we were the Davenports.

The man introduced himself as Wade Harris and told us that he would take us to the ship by limo. Impressed, I gave Jonathan the thumbs up. "Wow you spared no expense."

"This is our honeymoon and nothing but the best for my wife."

I nudged him affectionately, "Hey, I like the way you say *my wife*."

Placing my head on his shoulder, I looked out the window as we headed to Port Canaveral to board the ship. I had never been to Florida before, and felt jitters of excitement as I noted the colorful homes and buildings and the exotic plants and greenery that I'd never seen before. I was fascinated by the ocean and we could have driven around Florida forever as far as I was concerned. However, in what seemed like a few short minutes we were pulling up to a parking lot near where the ship was docked.

The line moved fast. Before we knew it, we were given our boarding passes and were allowed to board the ship. The Captain greeted each passenger with a smile and a saying "Welcome aboard" After finding our cabin and getting settled, we decided to go to the upper deck for some entertainment.

The music from the calypso band was loud, but the beat was good. There were plenty of the people on their feet dancing. Others were sitting around talking, eating and drinking at the numerous bars. Jonathan pointed to the sliding doors, so we walked over and they automatically opened. When we walked in, it was nice and cold. Plenty of people were sitting and eating, all different kinds of foods. The choices ranged from sandwiches and chips, or fries, pizza and salads. We decided on the pizza and tossed salad.

Jonathan and I found a table for two near a window where we could eat and people watch until the ship sailed. I enjoyed every minute. After lunch, we decided to find our cabin. When we arrived we noticed that our luggage was not in the front of our door yet. We saw people walking with life jackets, so we stood still, allow them to pass and there was an announcement about a safety class, Jonathan and I decided to pass. Since he had been on a cruise before he said that he knew where to locate the life jackets.

"And anyway, he added, If the ship goes down, I would definitely save you."

After hearing that I felt so secured. So, we explored the ship to see what other activities were offered. There were several nightclubs, a casino and a large stage where comedy and Broadway acts would be performed. We even stumbled upon an exercising room with a spa.

We went back to our cabin to unpack. Jonathan had spared no expense when it came to our living quarters. There was a small seating area, and he had arranged for the delivery of a vase filled with a dozen, beautiful red roses which had been placed on the coffee table. The bed was queen-size. There were two plush robes resting on it. The ocean side cabin even had a private balcony, complete with two lounge chairs so that we could make ourselves comfortable.

Jonathan slid the doors to the balcony open and he and I stepped outside to see the ocean.

Two hours later, Jonathan and I had unpacked and were dressed for dinner. Arriving at the dinning room, we were escorted to our table. Two other couples were already seated. We introduced ourselves to Lydia and Donald Harrington from Texas and Etoria and Bill Winston, from Nashville, Tennessee. Like me, neither of the couples had been on a cruise before.

The six of us were deep in conversation when Jonathan started in surprise, catching my attention.

"What?"

"Look to your left. That looks like Becky and Ray Holiday entering the room.

I turned to see to whom he was referring and saw that they noticed us. They started walking in our direction. It was them, the Holidays. They had been members of Mount Goodwill Baptist Church for years. They were there before Jonathan became their minister.

Ray broke into a grin of recognition. "Pastor! So this is where you were taking Courtney on your honeymoon. This is our second cruise and boy, are you both going to love it."

Jonathan seemed happy to see them "What are you two doing here? Did you bring the children?"

Becky answered. "The children are with our parents, and this trip is for my birthday present."

"Lucky you," I smiled up at Becky, happy for her good fortune. It was hard to believe that she was fifty years old. The mother of three girls, she kept her body in tip-top condition and dressed to kill. Both she and her husband were stylish dressers, and outgoing personalities.

"We're sitting three tables over." Ray pointed across the room. "After dinner, why don't you two meet us on the upper desk to sit, talk and even take in the night air?"

Jonathan spoke for both of us. "Courtney and I would love to meet you there. See you later."

We arrived at the upper deck, looking for Becky and Ray, but we couldn't locate them. We decided to find a table of four and sit and wait. The band was playing and people were dancing and enjoying themselves. We heard a shout and looked and saw them in a line doing the electric slide. Becky was laughing out loud and not missing a step. Ray was behind her on the second line watching and dancing as if this was either his first time or he wasn't too familiar with the steps.

The music finally stopped and they came to join us. Becky said she was so happy to be away from the children. Her plans were to have big fun. We just smiled and I told her look like she was off to a good start. She asked if I wanted to meet her in the morning to exercise. I told her no. I was on my honeymoon and didn't want to make any appointments early in the morning. I told her we were in a suite and I just may stay in and order room service for breakfast.

The band played another song and they were asking people to join in a long dance line around the deck. Jonathan and I refused, but Becky and Ray jumped to the chance. While they were in the line laughing and dancing, I waved bye to Becky. I told Jonathan this is a good time to exit and go to our cabin to be alone.

I woke up when I heard a knock on our cabin door. Through my sleepy eyes I saw Jonathan taking a tray of food.

I was stretching and yawning when Jonathan said, "Good morning sleepy head. I got up early and ordered breakfast, so when you got up it will be here."

"Well, you timed it just right! I wasn't sound asleep. I was just laying here, thanking God for being on this ship. Also, thanking Him for you. You have given me the time of my life."

"You're more than welcome. I want you to look back and remember this time with a smile."

"I'm going to wash my face, brush my teeth, and have a word of prayer. I won't be long, so why don't you take the tray on the balcony, so we can eat out there."

When I came out of the bathroom, Jonathan had everything setup. We held hands and had a word of prayer. Afterward, he kissed me and said, "I love you Mrs. Davenport"

I smiled and said, "I love you Jonathan Davenport."

After breakfast, Jonathan and I got dressed and in no time we were exiting the ship. We were greeted by plenty of waiting cabs to take passengers around the island. Jonathan and I decided to walk for the exercise.

As we walked, the first thing we saw was a group of island ladies braiding hair. They would braid tourist hair for money. One of the ladies wanted me to get my hair braided, but I didn't want it done. Jonathan said this was their way of making a living, so he gave the lady some money anyway.

We continued walking and there were vendors on both sides of the streets. We stopped and purchased some t-shirts for the boys. When we walked a little further a colorful handbag, with a matching wallet made of straw caught my eye. I just had to purchase it for Darlene.

Jonathan and I went into the jewelry shop looking at the different cuts of diamonds. He wanted to purchase me a diamond tennis bracelet, but I told him no. I have plenty of diamonds. I did notice a grocery store on the corner. I suggested we visit there and purchase some cold water.

Since it was so hot, Jonathan was all for that. We walked in looking at all the different kinds of island food. I wondered down the spice aisle. It was something to see all of the spices with names I couldn't pronounce.

Jonathan found a barrel filled with ice and bottles of water. He grabbed two from the bottom. When he gave the cashier the money, she opened the drawer. I looked in and saw that they had their own currency. I thought that was odd because she took our United States dollars.

Jonathan said he was getting a little tired. I gave him the bags and asked him to take a seat in the shade, while I walk to the ladies shop to get a bathing suit. When I came out, he wasn't there. I walked back to the grocery store and he wasn't in there either. When I got back to where we purchased the t-shirts for the boys, he was standing there with a big smile on his face.

"Jonathan I've been all over this island looking for you."

"I sat for what seemed like an hour. Then I thought you may have forgotten where you left me, so I walked to the ladies shop, but you were gone. I got a bright idea to backtrack. I went back to the grocery store, but you weren't there either. I even went to the jewelry store. I was about to give up, and head to the ship, when I saw you walking in my direction."

"Jonathan, what do you mean head for the ship? This is no place to leave a lady." He started laughing as if he was up to something but I didn't see the humor in it at all.

Chapter Eight

After Jonathan and I packed the souvenirs purchased for the boys and for our friends, I felt a little tired. In Freeport, we had shopped until we dropped. We sampled island delicacies and met more new people than I could count.

I knew a good hot shower would rejuvenate me. After the long shower, I entered the room to find Jonathan fast asleep. I sat on the bed beside him. The movement woke him. I kissed him softly on his lips.

"Hey, was I in there that long?"

He turned toward me. "No, I was waiting on you to come out. I laid across the bed and must have fallen asleep." He raised a corner of my pillow. "Courtney, what is that under there?"

Curious, I picked up the pillow to see what he was talking about. Laying there was a long box wrapped in gold paper. It was tied with a big white bow. "Jonathan, what is in this?"

"I guess you have to just open it and see."

I couldn't get it opened fast enough. It was the diamond tennis bracelet that I had looked at when we were shopping in Freeport. He had asked me if I wanted it, but I felt that it was too expensive. I was overjoyed.

"Jonathan! Oh, Jonathan! You are too good to me." I nearly knocked him over. I leaped into his arms so hard. "You got the bracelet. It's so beautiful!"

"I knew it would look better on you than in the case." He placed it on my wrist.

I admired the sparkling stones. "You were right, it's so beautiful!" I covered his face with kisses. "Oh, Jonathan, thank you so much!"

I had the most wonderful husband in the world. Even our overnight at the Atlantis, which was located on Paradise Island, Bahamas, was paradise. After a day exploring the island, we enjoyed a delicious dinner, followed by a comedy show at the hotel. The comedian was funny and his jokes were clean. He had the entire audience laughing.

I don't know which I enjoyed more, the activities off the ship or onboard the ship, and the onboard activities were nonstop. As a minister and as his wife, there was a lot of partying in which we would not engage, but it didn't stop the fun that we had.

The last day onboard, I woke up and looked around only to find Jonathan in the living room reading his Bible. He smiled at me.

"Good morning."

"Good morning, why didn't you wake me, so we could get an early start in getting off the ship?"

"I was just looking at you sleeping. You looked so peaceful. I decided to get my Bible and start reading and praising God for another day."

"Well, I see you're ready to go, so I better get up and get ready. I promise not to be too long."

"Good idea, and when you come out of the bathroom, I'd like to talk to you about something."

After bathing, I felt relaxed. Breakfast from room service was waiting for me, so before dressing, Jonathan and I enjoyed our last meal aboard the ship. It was delicious.

I had dressed and was checking the room for anything we might have forgotten to pack, when I remembered that Jonathan wanted to talk to me. I questioned him about it and what he said was the last thing on earth I expected to hear.

"Courtney I'm so happy to have you as my wife, but I also want you to think about quitting your job."

"Quitting my job?" I was stunned. "Jonathan, I have worked too hard to get where I am. Hard work does pay off. You see that my company allowed me transfer from Chicago back to Indianapolis. I can't just walk off my job! They've been too good to me."

"Courtney, hear me out. What I'm saying is that our church has two thousand members and fifteen hundred of them are active. We have two services, and I just feel that all of the responsibility that comes with being a minister's wife on top of trying to support me and take care of the boys, all might be too hard on you. Look at me. I was working at Ford until last year. When our congregation grew so strong that I couldn't handle both, I was told to resign. The church needed a full-time Pastor."

I was deeply distressed. He couldn't be serious. "Jonathan let me think about it. I know I'm working on a project now and I will have to get it completed. Maybe I'll look into cutting my days or working part-time. You know I want to support you and be a good mother to the boys."

"Courtney, I just feel you're one person and trying to do it all will mean that something will eventually be lacking. I know from experience with Deborah how tough it can get. That's why she stopped working. It got to be too much for her."

"Jonathan we'll talk about this when we get back home."

He agreed, and we prepared to leave from the ship. The fun that we had on our honeymoon had quickly become a thing of the past. As we walked down the gangplank headed back home, all I could think about was Jonathan comparing me to his deceased wife, Deborah.

My main objective was Jonathan and the boys, and I would do all I could to earn the respect of the congregation, but it was best for everyone, including my husband, to remember, that I am not Deborah Davenport. I'm Courtney, Courtney Davenport!

Chapter Nine

Back in Indianapolis, we claimed our luggage, and hauled them along with our souvenirs outside to the pickup area to wait for our ride. The honeymoon was over and now back to reality.

I was happy to be home. I had so much to tell Morgan about our trip. I had called her on our return to Florida and she had promised to pick us up at the Indianapolis airport. She timed it just right. Jonathan and I were just pulling our luggage to the curb, when Morgan drove up. Her fiancé, Christopher, was with her. Leaping out of the car, she greeted me as if I had been gone for a year.

"Sis I miss you so much! It seems like you two have been gone for such a long time."

After greeting Christopher, I hugged my sister tightly. "I missed you too, little sis. I can't wait to tell you about our trip." I felt excited all over again simply thinking about our honeymoon.

Morgan helped us put the bags in the car. "Why don't you two get settled first, then I can come over tomorrow and hear all about the trip."

"Sounds good to me, but why not wait until we get the pictures developed, that would be even better." The four of us got into the car and headed toward the highway. "I know! Sunday afternoon Jonathan can cook out and we can share the pictures with you and Christopher then."

"Sounds good to me, but tell us a little about it while I am driving."

I knew that Morgan was too curious not to want to know something. "Well I can tell you that we had a great time. We met some very nice people and boy, did we eat!"

"That's what I hear. I hope one day Christopher and I can take a cruise."

Christopher chuckled. "Morgan, are you asking me to take you on a cruise for our honeymoon?"

"I didn't say it had to be our honeymoon, but if you do and from the looks on Courtney and Jonathan's face I know I would absolutely love it."

"All right, I wanted to save this as a surprise, but I was thinking about taking you either on a cruise or to Hawaii, when the time came."

Morgan squealed. "Christopher, don't make me have an accident. You know how much I want to go to Hawaii. Now stop kidding with me, but seriously, we can start making some plans to get our trip booked."

The three of us laughed. Morgan was something else.

As we continue driving along quietly, my thoughts turned to John. I sure hoped that Jonathan wasn't making plans to pick him up tonight, Monday would be soon enough. I needed time to prepare myself before that happened.

As Morgan pulled up in the front of our home, I was feeling a little nervous. This was to be the beginning of my new life with John. I took a deep breath and got out the car. Jonathan and Christopher handled the luggage. I was about to follow them up the steps and into the house when Morgan stopped me. She looked serious.

"Courtney, this is your house now. Deborah is dead and you are now Jonathan's wife. Go on in and make yourself comfortable. Please don't let John take your joy."

I smiled at her. She has always been my rock. I then said to her, "You're right. I promise to be just as happy here as I was on the ship. Whether he likes it or not, I am now his stepmother."

"That's right, and if he want his days to be long he'd better do as it says in Ephesians 6:1,2 and 3, *Children obey your parents in the Lord; for this is right. Honor thy father and mother; which is the first commandment with promise; That it may be well with thee, and thou mayest live long on the earth.*"

"Preach little sister! Now come on inside and get the souvenir that I brought from the islands. I even got something for Christopher."

After getting their souvenirs, Morgan and Christopher rushed off, realizing that it was our first night in our home. Jonathan called and spoke with the boys while I was unpacking my clothes. He told them that he would pick them up tomorrow afternoon. He made a call to John. I heard him ask if he wanted to come home Sunday after church. He went on to tell him that he was going to grill outside and have a few family members over to show off our pictures. I heard Jonathan then say, if it was all right with his grandparents it was okay with him.

After he disconnected, Jonathan informed me that John was going to stay another week with his grandparents. I had to admit that in my heart I was shouting *thank you Jesus for a few more days of peace.*

Later, Jonathan went to buy takeout, while I set the table. I found some candles and holders, placed them in the center of the table and lit them. Then I dimmed the lights to make it romantic.

When Jonathan came back with the food, I placed it in crystal serving dishes and Jonathan and I dined. As I sat across the table from my husband, I was happy as any new bride could be. I knew in my heart that this was a marriage made in heaven. With God as our foundation, we were going to be a very happy couple, with or without John.

I woke up to the smell of bacon. Jonathan had prepared hash-browned potatoes, bacon, biscuits.

I'm not a big eater, especially breakfast, but it did look good, so I ate heartily.

After breakfast I finished unpacking boxes while Jonathan went to pick up the two youngest boys.

As I looked around the house, I knew, eventually, I was going to change things to my liking. This had been Deborah's house, now it belonged to me.

I went upstairs to the boys' room. Each had a room of their own. David's was decorated with cartoons characters. They were on the bedspread and curtains. Dwayne's room was similar, except that he was a Star Wars fan. I left the souvenirs that I brought them on each of their beds.

Entering John's room, I was impressed with how neat he kept it. The queen-size bed was neatly made. There was no clutter anywhere. There were pictures of football players and rap artists on his walls, and everything was decorated in the color of blue, a peaceful color. How ironic.

Looking out of John's bedroom window, I saw

Jonathan's car pull into the driveway. I got downstairs in time to see the door and in walked my two young men. The three of us grinned at each other. David was holding six roses wrapped in green paper and Dwayne had a box of chocolates. Shyly, they handed me their gifts.

I thanked them both and gave them big hugs and kisses. I told them that after they took their luggage to their rooms we are going out to dinner. Delighted, they rushed upstairs. Jonathan was just as pleased as the boys.

"What a nice surprise. I know they are going to like that. Where are we going?"

"Red Lobster."

"Good, that's one of our favorite places."

Jonathan hesitated, and I knew that there was something else on his mind. I waited.

"Baby, the boys and I had a little discussion about what they feel comfortable calling you. They want to call you Momma Courtney, if it's okay with you. Now, if you don't like that, we can come up with something else to make you more comfortable."

"Oh Jonathan I love that. But, what about John?"

"Look, we'll deal with John when he comes home. Let's just enjoy the two boys and not worry about him until he's here. He's a good kid. He'll come around."

Jonathan gave me a kiss and a hug. We looked up and the boys were coming into the room. They were thrilled about all the gifts I'd left on their beds. The look on their faces made me feel happy inside.

"Boys, Momma Courtney and I would like to take you to Red Lobster."

They looked at each other and yelled "Red Lobster!" The rush to the front door told us that we had picked the right place.

Chapter Ten

I eased out of bed trying not to wake Jonathan. I know he had a restless night. I couldn't help but notice how much he tossed and turned. I think that he was concerned about John coming home. I know I was.

I almost made it completely out the room, but when I looked over my shoulder, Jonathan was putting his feet on the floor.

"What time is it?"

"It's early, Jonathan, too early to get up. You have a little more time to sleep. You don't have to preach today, so lay back down. I'm going to get breakfast. I'll come back and wake you and the boys."

Before I completed my sentence he was back in the bed with the sheet over his head. I smiled and quietly left the room.

Entering the kitchen, I looked around at the white walls and white curtains and shook my head. I would definitely have to go shopping to put some kind of color in this kitchen.

I wanted our first breakfast together to be a nice one, so I planned on cooking pancakes, sausage and scrambled eggs. I turned the radio on to keep me company. Aretha Franklin was singing one of my favorite songs "Amazing Grace" It held a message for me. I know that's for sure that

God's grace is amazing, and it was His grace that was going to keep me while I took on the task of raising three boys.

"Good morning Momma Courtney. I smell sausage"

I startled, it was David. "Oh! You frightened me, Good morning David and yes you do smell sausage. Have you washed your face and brushed your teeth?"

"Not yet, the smell brought me down here, but it won't take me but a minute. I'll go and wake Dwayne. I know I'll have to call him a million times. He is so hard to get out of bed, especially on a Sunday morning."

"Thanks and on your way upstairs, please peek in our room and tell your father breakfast is almost ready."

Everyone enjoyed breakfast which was filled with conversation and lots of laughter. The boys sure did know how to make me feel good. All during breakfast they all kept saying how good everything tasted complimenting my cooking. I just smiled and watched them clean their plates.

After breakfast, we got ready for church, since Jonathan wasn't preaching he would be sitting with the boys and me in the pews

I was a little nervous thinking about this being the first Sunday that I entered the church as his wife. The boys wore their best suits instead of pants and shirts. I think they knew that all eyes were going to be on us as the first family and they wanted to look good.

I must have changed clothes a dozen of times. I finally settled on my linen navy and white suit. I had a beautiful large brim navy hat that matched my shoes and purse. Looking at myself in my floor length mirror, I really liked what I saw. I looked the part of a first lady.

When I joined them in the family room, claps and whistles from Jonathan and the boys greeted me. Before leaving for the church we had a word of prayer.

The ride to church was quiet. On our arrival, Jonathan parked in his spot marked Pastor. He came to my car door to help me out. The boys were already standing in the front of the car waiting for us to walk in together. The choir was ready to march in, but they waited for us. We were greeted with kind words, hugs, and kisses.

The organist was softly playing. The ushers opened the doors. Jonathan, the boys and I walked in. We were greeted with love. The congregation gave us a standing ovation. I was on top of the world. After we were escorted to our seats the service began.

Minister Holland was a dedicated preacher who had been a member of our church for over twenty years. He was going to deliver the message of the day. He's the kind of preacher, who preaches on fire and brimstone. He will tell you heaven or hell and no in between.

The service went as usual. The choir did a good job. Minister Holland sermon was the Bait of Satan. He talked about how Satan will come at you in all kind of disguises. He gave an example of being single. How Satan would send a man into your life sharply dressed from head to toe. He would also know just the right words to say to get your attention. He will catch you at your weakest point and sure enough you will fall for the bait. He said, but if you stay prayed up, you will be able to recognize his traps. He went on and on with sweat falling from his brow, he was preaching and people were talking back. Before he ended his sermon he asked a question and took his seat. Ten people young and old ran up the aisle to accept Jesus as their personal savior and to be a member of the church.

One lady came running up the aisle with tears streaming down her face, she held up both hands and said, "I need to join because Minister Holland asked a question that was just for me. He said if Christ came today, where would you spend eternity? I took this personally because you see, I'm over fifty years old and I'm sick and tired of the streets. I was born and raised in the church. I've been baptized and know scriptures from Genesis to Revelations and all in between."

One man stood and said "Testify my sister. Let God use you."

She wiped her tears and continued talking to Minister Holland. She said, "But somewhere in my life I met a man and he turned me away from Christ. I took the bait, but this day, I'm turning my life over to Christ! I didn't know why I came here today, but now I do. I came to give my life back to Christ. I'm going home to tell that man, that no good man, who is not my husband to get out! Today, I'm leaning and trusting in God." She looked at Minister Holland, took his hand and said. "If Christ comes now, I know where I will spend eternity."

When that lady started shouting and screaming. Most of the congregation was shouting back and there wasn't a dry eye in the place. The Spirit of the Lord filled the sanctuary, and I knew in my heart that whatever trials I might face with Jonathan's oldest son, in the end, everything would be all right.

Chapter Eleven

The church service ended and we were covered by a mass of people welcoming Jonathan and me from our honeymoon. I saw Mrs. Jessup walking in our direction and I wanted to leave, but people had me blocked in. She rushed to where I was standing and interrupted a conversation I was having. She pushed a young man who she had dragged along with her forward.

"Excuse me Courtney, this is my grandson and he thinks he knows you."

Despite her rudeness, he stood there politely so I reached out to shake his hand. There was something familiar about him, but I couldn't remember where we had met before, but he had a sly grin like his grandmother's.

"My name is Ronald Jessup and I used to take pictures for the school newspaper. Didn't you graduate from Indiana University?"

"Yes."

"Are you sure you don't remember me?"

I looked at him closely, but I gently said, "No, but it certainly was nice meeting you, and thanks for worshipping with us today."

Mrs. Jessup was so adamant about me knowing her grandson, that my only thought was what is this woman up to now?

Other members came rushing to where Jonathan and I were standing and the next thing I knew Ronald and his grandmother were easing away.

Jonathan, the boys, and I were finally able to leave. The cookout was in a few hours and there was a lot to do.

When we got home we changed into our comfortable clothes. The boys helped to ice down the pop, while Jonathan fired up the grill. I started heating the green beans and warming the bake beans.

Morgan and Christopher were the first to arrive. Christopher went outside to be with Jonathan while Morgan and I put the dessert they brought out on the kitchen counter. She had purchased a pound cake, a cherry cobbler, strawberry cheesecake and a deep dish pecan pie. I wanted to ask her why so much, but when I looked out the window, I saw all of the cars pulling up, I knew that she had brought just enough.

Morgan went outside to be with Christopher, and a short while later Mom and Granny came into the kitchen.

Mom had brought devil eggs, potato salad and a bowl of corn. I kissed her and thanked her for pitching in.

Granny looked at me and said, "I know I didn't bring anything but don't I get a kiss?"

"Of course." I reached over and hugged her tightly, then kissed her on the cheek.

My grandmother is eighty-six-years-old and just as feisty as ever. Leaving Mom and me in the kitchen to talk, she left us to explore the house. Mom and I had a short conversation about John. She told me to be patient with him and by all means stay prayerful. I promised her that I would. Granny returned to offer her opinion on what she had observed.

"You sure do have a nice house, Courtney, but why don't you get rid of that piano you can't play. I remember when your mother tried to get you to take lessons but you didn't want too. Morgan did and she has talent to sing and play."

Mom knew that Morgan has always been Granny's favorite grandchild, so she suggested that she and Granny go outside. I was happy that they did because I didn't need her on my case today. That was one reason that I didn't invite Mrs. Jessup. She was just as nosey as Granny.

Darlene walked in with a large pot of collar greens, a pan of cornbread and two sweet potatoes pies. This small cookout had turned into a large gathering of family and friends. We brought all the food outside and spread it on the table so that we could eat buffet style.

After my father blessed the food, we sat together and talked and ate some more. Eventually, I got out the honeymoon album and passed it around. There were lots of fun comments about the expressions on our faces showed that we were indeed having the time of our life. Even Granny had some nice things to say about the pictures.

It was getting dark and all of the working people were saying how it was time to call it a night.

Everything was cleaned up. Goodbyes were said, and I went straight to my deep jet bathtub for a much needed bath. I placed my favorite candles around the tub, laid back, and enjoyed the hot relaxing water gently caressing my tired body.

When I came out of the bathroom, entered the bedroom, Jonathan wasn't in bed. I could hear him in his office on the phone. I didn't want to disturb him, so after I prayed I got into bed. Shortly after, Jonathan joined me. He looked preoccupied.

"Is everything all right?" I was concerned.

"It isn't anything for you to worry about. Just go to sleep."

He wasn't going into details, so I didn't push him. Wrapped in his arms, I fell fast asleep. Yet, I felt in my spirit that something wasn't right.

Chapter Twelve

I was happy about going back to work. I looked at my watch and noticed it was a little too early to clock in, so I exited off the interstate for Long's bakery. Everyone in our small office loved donuts from Long's Bakery, so I purchased some as a surprise. When I walked in with the two bags of hot donuts, Julia Redding, the receptionist, rewarded me with a pleased smile. I smiled back.

"Good morning Julia."

"Good morning Courtney, or shall I say Mrs. Davenport." We hugged. "How was your honeymoon?"

"I had a beautiful honeymoon, but I'm happy to be back, even to the large stack of papers on my desk."

Julia looked surprised. "You don't know do you?"

"Know what?"

"We hired another person to help lighten your load."

"Lighten my load?" This time I was surprised. "Julia what's going on?"

"I think I've said more than I should. You go on to your office and see."

"Thanks I will." I gave her the donuts to place in the break room for me.

As I rushed to my office to see what in the world she was talking about. I heard my name being called. I stopped in my tracks and turned around. There stood, my boss, Mr.

East and a short petite lady with very short red hair. She had a narrow face, and a large smile.

"Good morning Courtney and welcome back."

"Thank you Mr. East."

"Courtney, this is Paula Raymond. She'll be working with you on some of your east side accounts."

With a smile as large as her's, I shook her hand in welcome, then excused myself. I went straight to my office and closed the door. I was steaming.

I have worked my butt off for this company. I'm the one who beat the pavement to get those east side accounts and now they were too much for me to handle? Sitting in my chair, I willed the tears not to flow. They did anyway.

I was wiping my eyes when there was a knock on the door.

"May I come in?" It was Julia.

"Yes, please do."

"Courtney, it wasn't my place to call you and tell you that Mr. East hired his best friend's daughter. Paula is straight out of college, I'm told that she knows the computer inside and out."

"It's okay, Julia. You're right! It wasn't your place to tell me. This is just an awful surprise. I came in so happy this morning and now to be hit with this. From what you're telling me, I bet she'll be the team leader soon and I'll be working under her."

Julia hesitated, and worried her bottom lip as if she had more to say, she did. "Courtney, I know you can keep a secret, Paula is dating Mr. East's son and I think that's really why he hired her. But, she's no slacker. She comes in early and works late. She's a regular team player. I think she wanted to learn the in and outs so that when you got back you would be impressed at how much she has learned about the company. She's good, but please don't let her intimidate you."

"I won't, I know this job and I do it very well! Now, I'm going into the break room for a donut and a cup of coffee."

"Now that's what I'm talking about! Come on, most of the gang is in there waiting to welcome you back."

I put my feeling aside and walked into the break room with my head high. I smiled and laughed with everyone.

After the morning break. I went back to my office to read my e-mails, some were work related and some were from friends. I laughed at most and deleted others. It was mid morning when I received a call from Jonathan. He wanted to know if I was free for lunch. I told him by this being my first day back I would have Julia pick up something for me and eat it at my desk. He understood and said there would be a surprise waiting for me when I get home. I thanked him and ended the call. I didn't tell him about Paula.

I spent the rest of the day working with the young woman, and going over some of the accounts with her. We spent time dividing up the accounts.

I was working so hard that I hadn't noticed that it was quitting time until Julia came into my office to see if I was ready to walk out with her. The parking lot was almost empty by the time we left.

"So what do you think about Paula?" Julia didn't hide her curiosity.

"I think that she's a hard worker and I feel she's going

to be good for the company."

"You think what? She practically got your job and that is all you can say, is she is a hard worker."

"I can't get angry with her. It was Mr. East who hired her."

"Well, I'm impressed with you. If it was my job that's almost being handed to the boss' future daughter-in-law, I would be angry and words would fly like feathers off of a chicken being plucked."

I laughed at her colorful description. "Julia I have a family at home to take care of now. This office used to be my life, but not anymore."

"So, are you going to quit?"

"No, I didn't say I was leaving the company, so don't go and tell that. I just said there isn't a thing I can do about Paula sharing my territory, so I'm going to have to live with it. See you in the morning."

"I'm not telling anything, If you quit that's your choice. Now get in your car and I will see you in the morning. Are you bringing donuts again?"

With that we each got into our cars and headed home.

Chapter Thirteen

As I drove home I passed several restaurants and thought about getting some carry outs, but then I thought about making something quick like hamburger helper, with green beans and dinner rolls.

I arrived home to find David and Dwayne playing basketball in the driveway. As I pulled into the garage beside Jonathan's car, the boys ran to meet me. They wanted to know how my day went. I told them as soon as I complete dinner. We would discuss our day at the dinner table.

When I walked into the family room, the surprise that Jonathan had promised me became quite apparent. He and John were sitting there watching TV. I didn't know if I should laugh or cry. I took a deep breath and walked into the room. Jonathan got up to meet me with a hug and a kiss. I walked over to where John was sitting and said "welcome home John, it's good to see you."

Without looking in my direction, he said "Hi."

I made a quick turn and went in the direction of our bedroom to get out of my suit and high heels. I put on my lounge dress and went into the kitchen to make some dinner. I asked Jonathan how he feels about hamburger helper. He said he liked it and so did the boys. I told him it wouldn't be too long for me to prepare dinner.

About an hour later, dinner was ready. Jonathan called

the boys. After he said the blessing, we started dinner and Jonathan asked about my day. I started telling him about Paula but before I completed my sentence John interrupted.

"What is this mess we're eating?" He frowned. "It tastes like Alpo dog food."

The two boys started laughing and I got up and ran into our bedroom. I found myself crying like I had lost my mother or father. It wasn't what he said, but how he said it. The expression on his face and how he threw the food down in his plate that made me upset. I guess when the boys took his side and laughed, that's what added fuel to the fire.

Jonathan came into the room and said, "Please don't pay any attention to John. I had a little talk with him before you came home. I guess it didn't do any good. I'm going to make him apologize and put him under a long punishment."

"Jonathan I shouldn't allow John to hurt me. I know he is trying to run me away and I refuse to let that happen."

"He is either going to eat what you cook or starve to death! We have had some nice days while he has been away and I'm not going to let him hurt you anymore. Now come back to the table and eat. We are a family."

When I went back, the two boys were still eating and holding their heads down, like they were sorry that they laughed at John's comment. Their plates were almost clean. David never looked up, but Dwayne told us that John threw his food in the trash, and stomped up the stairs to his room.

By this time I had no appetite. I sat and watched Jonathan finish his dinner. I was hurt by what had happened until I forgot the pie in the oven. It started to smell when Jonathan said something was burning. I remembered and rushed to the oven to find the cobbler boiling over onto the cookie sheet.

I didn't want any cobbler, so I took it to the table for them to enjoy. I went back into the kitchen. I could hear all the excitement coming from the dinning room. I knew the boys were happy about hot cobbler topped with vanilla ice cream. I smiled to myself knowing that John was probably upstairs wanting to come down to a bowl of cobbler.

I heard someone clear their throat, so I turned around. It was John standing in the doorway

"I'm sorry for what I said about dinner. Please accept my apology."

He wouldn't look at me. Instead, he looked down at the wooden floor. I told him he was forgiven. I also told him since he disturbed dinner there was no dessert for him. Sighing deeply, he turned and headed back upstairs to his room.

Jonathan came into the kitchen. He looked at me expectantly.

"John apologized for his action and I accepted it, but he still isn't getting dessert. This is my way of punishing him."

"Courtney, I'm with you all the way. When you punish the boys I'm going to be on your side. I refuse to let them play us against each other. We are one in this house."

The boys came into the kitchen with their dirty dessert bowls and both said how they cleaned their bowls. David said his bowl was so clean that I could just put it in the cabinet. I think he was telling me in a nice way, that if I prepare something like hamburger helper again, to make sure I have a tasty dessert to make up for a dinner in a box.

After dinner Jonathan went to go into his office to do a little reading and studying for his Sunday sermon. I went into the family room to read the Bible.

Just as I completed reading Isaiah 40, David slowly walked into the room with a book tucked under his arm.

"David, what you got there?"

"Momma Courtney, see my book I got from the library."

"Yes."

"Do you want me to read it to you?"

"Please, come and sit by me. I would love to know all about this story."

David started reading and after he completed a chapter, we would go back to discuss what he had read. I would pretend that he called the boy another name. He would look at me and correct me. This was my way of making sure he was reading with understanding.

The story started to hold my attention and the next thing I knew I wanted more. Lenny R. Howard was his name. He was shipped from one foster home to another. Finally he was placed in a loving home. What was unusual about this home was the parents were foster parents to eight other special need children, and yet they made room for one more.

Before I knew it, David was at the end of the book. It was a very interesting book about the life of Lenny. It took us from his adopted day, until the day he entered high school. We found out at the end that there was a sequel to the book. David said he was going back to the library to find it.

I thanked David for sharing his story. He hugged and kissed me before leaving the room. His actions towards me, made me feel loved and wanted again. I smiled to myself and said "God has a way that's mighty sweet."

Chapter Fourteen

I was sleeping soundly until a loud bolt of thunder woke me. A flash of lightning lit the room. I sat up in bed, looked over and noticed that Jonathan wasn't there. Putting on my robe, I walked through the house looking for him. I found him in his office on the telephone. The expression on his face let me know that something was wrong. Not wanting to disturb him, I slowly walked out and closed the door behind me.

By the time I got ready for work and fixed us a light breakfast, Jonathan entered the kitchen.

"Good morning." I gave him a light kiss on the lips.

"Good morning Honey, I've been on the phone with one of our members for the last hour."

"Oh yeah, who?"

"Sorry, it's private."

He took a sip of his coffee as if dismissing my question. That didn't sit well with me. I was just asking who in our church was having problems.

"Jonathan I don't understand. I know you told me that before we were married, but I'm your wife now. We should be able to share everything."

"No, not everything."

His words stunned and they hurt me. I left him sitting in the kitchen while I prepared to leave for work. My ride to work wasn't as good as usual. My mind was on his last statement "Not everything."

I pulled onto the parking lot the same time as Paula. She got out of her black BMW convertible. I smiled and said good morning. She did the same. We walked into the building without saying another word to each other. Julia greeted both of us with a smile. We both spoke and Paula walked toward the break room

"Hey Courtney, did you see Paula's new car? Julia's eyes were shinning with excitement. "She took me for a ride last week. We put the top down, and that's one smooth riding car. Hey, maybe she'll drive us to lunch today! Do you want me to ask her?"

"No, I have too much work to go out to lunch. I'll probably walk down to the side deli for a sandwich and eat at my desk, but thanks."

"You look like you have a lot on your mind this morning."

"Yes, I do, but I know the power of prayer, so I'll be okay."

"Do you want to talk about it?"

"No, Julia, but thanks"

I went to my office to get some much needed work done. Later, Paula joined me. We worked until lunchtime. She asked if I wanted to go out for lunch, but I declined her invitation. When she left my office I decided to call Jonathan. I didn't like how I left home feeling this morning.

I had just picked the phone up when Julia knocked on my door. She was standing there with a bouquet of fresh cut flowers. With a smile a mile wide, she placed them on my desk and left.

I couldn't get the attached card off fast enough. It read "It takes a man with a big heart to say I'm sorry, so I am saying it with a smile. I love you and please accept these flowers." Jonathan.

I smiled and dialed the church to let him know that he had made my day. I dialed his office, but the recorder came on. I tried home, but like the church, there was no answer. I thought *that's funny he should be either at church or home.*

Grabbing my purse, I left for the deli. When I walked outside there was Jonathan, leaning against his car. I was thrilled as I ran into his arms.

"I got the beautiful flowers and thanks."

"You're welcome. I didn't like the way you left the house this morning. I wanted you to understand that I do wear a lot of hats and that people want to make sure that they can trust me. If they think that they can't, then my congregation would never trust me. Do you understand what I'm saying?"

"Since you put it like that I do. I didn't like the way I left home either. I was a little upset and it made a horrible morning, but the flowers put a smile on my face. When I walked out and saw your car that made me feel even better. Would you like to walk to the deli for a sandwich with me?"

"That is why I came to take my lovely wife to lunch."

I flashed Jonathan a big smile. Suddenly, all of the work waiting for me on my desk was forgotten.

Then it hit me! "Hey, where are the boys?"

"Darlene wanted to take her children for pizza and a movie, so she went by the house and got the boys. She saw how I looked when I came into the office. She can read me like a book."

"Please tell Darlene thank you. Now come on and let's walk to the deli. I only have one hour for lunch." Jonathan reached for my hand and pulled me close to him, he then kissed me on the lips and we walked hand in hand towards the deli.

Chapter Fifteen

I got home and there was a note on the kitchen counter informing me that the boys had choir practice tonight. It also said that he hoped that I would be joining them at the church. I was dead tired. I said to myself *I'm going to sit this one out.* I went to our room, changed into shorts and a t-shirt, then curled up on the bed and went to sleep.

It was the slam of the bedroom door that woke me. I sat straight up. Jonathan turned on the light.

"We missed you at church."

"I was too tired."

"The boys and I went to Burger King and ate. Did you have something to eat?"

"No, not since lunch."

"Do you want me to go out and get you something?"

"No, I'll fix something. What time is it anyway?"

"Eight o'clock"

"Wow! That's late? I'd better grab something, get my shower and make it to bed. I have a long day tomorrow."

"Courtney, I know the boys are out for the summer and I don't mine cooking for them, but what are we going to do when school opens? You know they will have homework and you will need to have dinner ready early."

"Jonathan this is my first week back to work. When summer is over I plan to have a schedule we all can live by.

My main objective is to take care of you and the boys. So far, I think I'm able to handle work, home and church."

"Okay superwoman, we'll see."

Jonathan didn't look too pleased, so I blew him a kiss and left the room.

The next day was glorious and I had a full schedule waiting for me. Jonathan was up and the smell of hazelnut coffee brewing lured me into the kitchen. As I entered, I did not only see coffee, but orange juice and a bagel were also waiting for me to enjoy. I was pleasantly surprised.

"Good morning Jonathan"

"Good morning honey, I thought you would like to have a nice breakfast before you begin your hard day of work."

"This is very nice of you. I'll need the energy for all of the work I have waiting for me." I sat and gobbled down my breakfast. Jonathan looked concerned.

"Courtney, I don't want you to run yourself down. Like I said if this is going to be too much for you, let me know. I surely wouldn't want it to be us standing in your way."

"I know and I am going to give this my best shot. Like I said this company has been very good to me and I don't want to let them down. If it becomes too much we'll have to make some other arrangements."

Jonathan just looked at me and never said another word. You could tell from his facial expression that he figured it would be a waste of time to tell me about all I have on my plate. He would just let me fall flat on my face, so he can say I told you so. I knew tonight was Bible study and I was going to come straight home, cook and be ready to walk out with Jonathan and the boys.

Jonathan walked me to the car, kissed me and said for me to have a good day.

I rode to work listening to my morning gospel show. My mind wasn't on the lyrics, but on Jonathan. I was wondering could he be right. Could I actually do a good job at the office and at home? The conclusion was yes, I could. Like the Bible says, *I can do all things through Christ who strengthens me.*

The day moved swiftly, Paula and I spent the entire day at different office buildings meeting and greeting people. Paula was very professional. I was impressed by her knowledge of computers.

She and I made it back to the office a little before four o'clock. That gave me time to pick up something for dinner, go home, make the sides and have dinner ready before five thirty.

After picking up some ribs, I walked in looking for Jonathan and the boys. I could hear noise coming from upstairs, so I knew that the boys were in their rooms. I found Jonathan in his office typing on his personal computer.

"I'm home"

He didn't look up from the computer screen. "Hey, how was your day?"

"Paula and I did real well. We covered a lot of territory. She's excellent with the clients. I know she's going to do very well. What did you guys do today?"

"The boys and I hung around the house, but we are making plans to visit the zoo tomorrow. I told them it has been quite a while since I've been there. Afterward we thought we would have lunch at T. G. I. Friday's. Hey, would you like to take a late lunch and meet us there?"

"No, tomorrow will be just as busy as today, but maybe another time we all can do something fun together. I better get dinner ready, so you finish what you were doing and I'll call you to the table soon."

After changing from my work clothes, I put on an apron and whipped up the side dishes in no time. I called everyone to dinner. John was the first one to the table.

He said that something smelled good. I found myself smiling on the inside, but I wouldn't dare let him see how pleased I was by his comment. Jonathan said grace and we passed the serving plates. David even thanked me for preparing such a good meal.

I hated to disappoint him, but I forgot to get something sweet. My mind was on rushing home and making a delicious meal other than hamburger helper. Jonathan started a conversation about taking the boys school shopping. We were beginning to sound like a real family, and we got through the meal with no problems.

We talked about Saturday not being a good day, because the boys had a day camp to attend, so we settled on next Saturday. By them being away I knew this would give me time to look in their rooms to see what is mostly needed. Like under clothes, pants, shirts and shoes.

After dinner, John was the first to get up. He was about to leave the room, when Jonathan asked him to clean the table and load the dishwasher. John looked at me. I guess he thought I was going to say that I would do it, but I said what a good idea. I got up and went to the family room to do a little reading.

Chapter Sixteen

I said good morning to the Holy Spirit as I rushed to make it to work on time. When I came out the room Jonathan was sitting in the kitchen drinking a cup of coffee. He looked up with a smile.

"Courtney, you look very nice today"

"Thanks, I would have a cup of coffee with you, but we've got a staff meeting at eight o'clock. So I will see you this evening."

"Have a blessed day."

"You too, and you and the boys enjoy the zoo."

I leaned over and kissed him lightly, then rushed to my car. I had my usual morning drive to the office. My dial set to my favorite radio station, so I could listen to some much needed gospel music. I exited off the interstate only to find that I was now stuck in traffic. I kept inching up until I finally got to see the wreckage. There were two cars, but no one was hurt because both ladies were standing outside of the car with the police officer. One lady was pointing and fussing at the other. I didn't want to roll down my window to hear what the commotion was all about, so I drove on.

I arrived and noticed Julia wasn't in the reception area. While walking down the hall to my office, to get a notepad for the meeting, I over heard that Mr. East had merged with a company in Louisville. Also, that he was looking for someone in the Indianapolis office to head up a major project.

I walked into the boardroom and noticed everyone was already sitting with something to drink. I grabbed a cup of coffee and I took my seat just as Mr. East walked in.

"Good morning everyone, I am so happy that all of you could make it this morning. As you know this company is growing. We have the home office in Chicago, this office in Indianapolis, and now we have merged with one in Louisville, Kentucky."

All of us clapped and we looked around the room smiling at each other. We were all aware that he needed someone to go to Louisville and help set up. It was a plum assignment and everyone wanted it, including me.

"Again, I am so happy that our company is growing and I would like for Sylvia Murray to come into the office."

We all turned around. In walked a well dressed tall dark brown skinned lady, with long flowing hair. She had full lips and they were covered in red lipstick. She gave a welcoming smile.

"Everyone this is Sylvia, she's from the Chicago office. We have been very pleased with her work. We have a large project in the works, so she will be over that project. I would like for Paula and Courtney to drive down Monday to meet the staff. Paula and Courtney, please stand, so Sylvia can meet you."

We stood and introduced ourselves and then everyone at the table did the same. After the introductions, we sat around and discussed more about the new office, until the meeting was adjourned. I left the room for my office and it appeared as though Julia was on my heels. The moment I tried to close the door she knocked and walked in.

"Courtney, girlfriend, can you believe…."

I cut her off. "Julia! Not today! I'm in no mood for gossip. I have appointments on the east side. I have calls to make. I'm so busy that Paula has offered to fill in on some of my appointments."

"You better watch that *fill in* thing. I don't trust Paula, or shall I say the soon to be Mr. East's daughter-in-law."

"Julia, I thought you were impressed with her work ethics. What happened? Why do you dislike her now?"

"Okay, but I see what's happening here and you seem to be blind to it. She is only working hard to get your job!"

"Julia, you have your opinion and I have mine, but I'm not worried. What God has for me is for me, no devil in hell can take it away. Now I will talk to you later."

"Courtney, if I offended you I'm sorry, it's not my place to say anything. I'm going back to my desk and you have a good day."

I went and copied my contacts and walked them to Paula's office. I was about to knock when I saw Sylvia sitting in there. They were chatting and laughing like old friends. I backed off and went to my office and begin to suspect that Paula just may be up to no good.

Time had gotten away from me because I looked at the crystal clock on my desk and it read twelve o'clock. Julia came to see if I wanted to go out, but I had to refuse her. I told her I would grab some chips and get ready for my afternoon appointments.

Later, Paula came in and was ready for the afternoon

appointments. We met with the company and had training on the new software. While I was working with the managers, she took it upon herself to show a small group the new product.

We worked so hard that when we came from the last meeting it was time to call it a day. When I drove Paula back to the office, she wanted to go in and do some paperwork. I decided to get home to Jonathan and the boys.

While driving home I couldn't help but to wonder why, Paula decided to continue to work, when we had already completed so much during the work day. Once again, I became suspicious.

When I arrived home David and Dwayne were in the driveway playing basketball. I didn't see Jonathan's car.

David welcomed me with a hug and kiss. He knew just how to make me feel good. Dwayne was still shooting hoops, but he did stop to say hello. He told me that Jonathan was at the church and John was upstairs on his computer.

After changing clothes, I went upstairs to say hello. I looked between the cracked door and I saw that he was on his computer.

"John I'm home."

He jumped and clicked his mouse, then turned to face me looking guilty. It looked as if I had caught him doing something he had no business doing. Then he got an attitude.

'What are you doing sneaking up on me?"

I just wanted to let him know that I was home and that dinner would be ready shortly. I turned to leave the room, but decided that I refused to let him use that tone of voice with me.

"For the record, I wasn't sneaking up on you." I turned and walked out before I said more. What he doesn't know is that I'm a computer wizard. I planned on coming back to his room one day when he isn't home, log on to his computer and see what had him so nervous when I came into his room.

By the time I went back downstairs, Jonathan was home. He looked good, dressed in a nice short-sleeved light blue shirt and tan casual pants. He appeared to be in a good mood.

"Hey, how was your day?"

"It was good. Mr. East merged with our new office in Louisville. He wants Paula and me to drive there Monday."

"What?" The good mood quickly vanished.

"Jonathan, before you get bent out of shape, it's only for one day. It's not an overnight trip. We'll be home before dark."

"Courtney, you have a family now. I think this job is getting to be too much for you to handle. I notice that the boys and I are eating later and later each night. What are you going to do when school opens?"

By now I am getting a little frustrated with him. We have had this conversation in the past. "Jonathan, I will make a schedule that all of us are able to live with. I told you, if this is too much I would look into cutting my hours."

"Okay, I will let you handle it."

"Courtney, don't forget the ladies worship meeting tomorrow night. Darlene wanted me to remind you because this is only the second meeting."

"Jonathan thank you, I really did forget about it. I'll be there. Now give me a few more minutes and dinner will be ready."

Chapter Seventeen

"Courtney! Courtney! The alarm clock has gone off twice. It's time for you to get up. You're going to be late"

I heard the word late and boy did my feet hit the floor running. I kept thanking Jonathan for waking me. I got dressed so fast, it surprised me. I took one final look and headed to the kitchen, where I knew Jonathan would be sitting. He was doing just that, sitting with a cup of hot coffee in one hand and the newspaper in the other. I didn't see a cup for me. So, I just kissed him on the forehead and said, "Have a good day."

I walked to the car as fast as my legs could carry me, wondering if the lack of coffee and breakfast had something to do with me not being able to handle the job and home. I was in no mood to discuss that subject again.

When I arrived at the office, I didn't see Paula's car. That was unusual. Her car was usually one of the first cars on the lot. I walked in and Julia was at her desk. She gave me a cheerful hello. I returned her greeting and walked to my office. I had some software testing to do and knew that it would take a full day.

I went into the kitchen for my coffee, water and orange juice. I was in no mood for the bagels that were sitting next to the coffee. I kept thinking about the look on Jonathan's face when I walked out. When I get home I will set the clock ten minutes fast and turn the volume up, so he won't have to call me over and over again.

Paula came into my office, she was neatly dressed as always, but this time instead of her wearing a pantsuit, she had on a dress.

"Good morning Paula, why the dress?"

"Good morning Courtney, I will be meeting some important friends after work and I wanted to look nice."

"Well, you will impress them with your black and white dress with matching checkered shoes."

"Thanks, I'm excited about our trip Monday aren't you?"

"Yes, I think Sylvia will show us a nice time in Louisville."

"What did your husband say about the trip?"

"I told him it is only for one day, so he was comfortable with it."

"I see you have been in the kitchen, so I better get me a cup of coffee and start testing the new software."

"Okay, I'm doing a lot of testing myself. If we discover any new problems, why don't we meet in my office and go over our findings. Let's say about two o'clock."

"Okay, see you later."

I spent most of the day working non-stop. Julia was nice enough to bring me a taco salad from the deli down the street. I stopped long enough to eat it and wash it down with a glass of diet coke.

Two o'clock Paula came into my office. We compared notes and made some changes. She went back to her office, while I returned to the training room to do a little more testing.

About an hour or two later, Mr. East came into the room. From the expression on his face either he was excited or had some good news to share.

"Courtney, I dropped in to say thank you for letting Paula do the thirty minute presentation on the new software. I must say, she did an excellent job! She said you were too busy, and thought that it would be a great opportunity for her. I'm so proud that you two work so well together. Carry on, I don't mean to stop the progress."

I couldn't smile, or open my mouth. I just let him take the floor, but I'm so confused. I never gave Paula permission to do a thirty minute presentation. The new software still has a few bugs to work out and she is aware of this. What is Mr. East talking about?

I rushed to Paula's office to find her sitting at her desk writing. "Paula, I need to speak with you."

I closed her door lightly and stood, I was too angry to take a seat. "Paula, Mr. East just left the training room. He said I gave you permission to do a thirty minute presentation. Is this true?"

"Well, you were too busy to handle it, so I thought I would help you out by presenting it on your behalf."

"My behalf? Paula, I didn't know anything about this presentation."

"I thought I might have mentioned it in passing."

This time she has really pushed my buttons. Now she is trying to make me look stupid. I yelled, "I am so tired of John, Mrs. Jessup and now your mess! You lying witch! How can I give you permission about something that I didn't have knowledge of?"

"What are you talking about and what did you call me?"

"You heard me, a lying witch."

"Courtney, calm down. We must stay professional. I didn't do anything wrong so the name calling should stop! Besides, you should appreciate my kindness."

"Kindness, your kindness is for your own benefit."

"Okay, I'm sorry for what I did. I am willing to stay late and work on the software."

"I thought you had some important friends to meet after work."

"I'll just call to let them know that something came up, we will just have to reschedule it."

I was about to say to her I feel this is another lie, she was dressed up for the presentation, but I thought about how close she has pushed me to the edge already. I took a deep breath and told her I was sorry for the name calling, please forgive me. I didn't wait for her to accept my apology or reject it. I just turned and went to my office to call it a day.

While riding home I kept thinking this is the worse day of my life! I can't believe the lie that Paula told to Mr. East. Now she has me wondering how many more lies have been told.

I pulled into the grocery store lot and ordered two large meat lovers pizzas, and some breadsticks. I knew that I had to meet the ladies at seven o'clock. I rushed in to get some punch and cookies to go with dinner. I had no time to make a hot dessert tonight.

While pulling in the drive, I said a little prayer because I didn't want Jonathan to know what happened today. I looked around and noticed that the boys weren't outside. I went inside and found Jonathan in his office working on the computer.

I leaned over and gave him a kiss. "Hey, what are you doing?"

"I'm working on my sermon for Sunday. How was your day?"

I swallowed my tears, so he wouldn't see the disappointment in my face. I did not want him to assume that I am unable to fulfill my duties at work and at home. "Very busy, but we got it all taken care of. Since I'm going to that meeting at church tonight, I ordered pizza and breadsticks. I hope everyone likes meat lovers."

"Yes. Do I need to pick it up?"

"No, they'll deliver it. Do you want me to make you a salad to go with your pizza?"

"No, we'll eat just what you ordered."

"I'm going upstairs to say hello to the boys. I'll come and get you when the pizza is delivered."

I went upstairs. John was on his computer. I just said hello and walked on. Dwayne was looking at television and so was David. I told them I ordered pizza and when the doorbell rings, to come down for dinner.

I changed into my comfortable lounge dress and slippers. I set the table and just as I was about to put ice in the glasses the bell rung. The pizza was delivered and the boys came running to the table like a herd of horses. David ran to get his father.

Jonathan was the last one to come to the table. The boys waited for him to bless the food. Hands were reaching for the pizza and breadsticks like they had never seen food before.

Friendly conversation filled the room, until Jonathan brought up the subject about a thirteen-year-old missing teenage boy. Jonathan started quizzing the boys about talking to strangers and not getting into their cars. He also told them it is much safer to walk in a group and not alone. For once John seemed to be listening and not showing off in the front of his two younger brothers. I was thinking maybe he realizes the seriousness because the missing teen was one year younger than him. I wanted to chime in, but I thought it would have been best for me to just sit and enjoy the pizza.

When dinner was over I reached for the glasses to put in the dishwasher and the paper plates in the garbage. I knew I had time to get dressed and make it to church about fifteen minutes early.

When I arrived there wasn't a car on the lot. All of that rushing was for nothing. I pulled into my reserved spot and took out my Sunday school book to do a little reading. I heard a car and looked over it was Darlene.

"Courtney, come on and let's go inside, the ladies will be here in about ten minutes."

"What is this all about?"

"This is a support group we started. It is to help women talk about their problems. This is our second meeting. We came up with a motto like I once heard 'what happens in Las Vegas, stays in Las Vegas'. So whatever we talk about, we should pray about it and not gossip. We start our devotion with scripture and prayer. We then open the floor by asking if someone had a particular problem or concern they wish to discuss."

"Last meeting one of the young ladies was dating a married man. She said in her eyesight there wasn't anything wrong with it, since he was separated from his wife. We had to pull out the scripture on her. Our words were kind, but firm. We explained to her about fornication and adultery. When we finished, she shed a few tears, but said she understood completely. She even called him from the church and told him to never call or come see her again."

"Wow! This support group is powerful. It seems to be just what we need. Is it open to women of all ages?"

"Yes, but mostly young ladies came. I'll say from about eighteen to fifty. You got to understand this is just our second meeting. The first meeting we had about fifteen women of all ages."

I helped Darlene pull some of the chairs in a large circle. We didn't know how many, so we pulled about twelve chairs. Just as I placed my Bible in a seat, the side door opened and the ladies were coming in. Darlene was right there were mothers, sisters and daughters walking in. They all were kind enough to greet me with a hug and a kiss.

Darlene took the floor. She thanked everyone for coming. She pointed to Lucinda and Shannon and asked them to read the scripture and to lead us in a word of prayer.

Marianne was a choir member, so she stared out singing a congregational song and we all joined in.

Lucinda stood and said, "I will bless the Lord at all

times; his praises shall continually be in my mouth." She then asked us to turn to Psalms 34 while she reads verses 1 through 8.

Shannon asked us to join hands while she takes us to the throne of grace. She said, "Dear Heavenly Father, we come to you because we have no other God to call on. We come to you with thanksgiving in our hearts. We come asking you to please forgive us for our sins. We ask you to please take care of each and every lady that is standing in this circle. Father you know our hearts, you know our concerns and you know all about our problems. Lord, we thank you for being the God that hears and answer our prayers. Lord we ask that you will continue to bless our families and church family. Lord please don't forget about the homeless, drug addicts and those who are behind prison walls. Lord thank you for you're many blessings. Let us all say amen."

Darlene took the floor again and thanked everyone for coming. The floor was opened for discussion. In walked Mrs. Jessup. It didn't take her long before she took the floor. She had plenty to say and it had nothing to do with what we were discussing. She said "Courtney, do you remember when I introduced you to my grandson Ronald?"

"Yes, I do."

"You acted as if you didn't know him then. Well, he remembers you, from Indiana University."

"And?"

"And he took a picture of you once standing in line with an application for a job."

She said it as if something had been wrong. "What's wrong with that?"

"The job was for Playboy magazine. Do you remember that?"

Darlene was so angry. She said "Mother Jessup, why would you bring up some dirt like this? The past is the past."

"No Darlene I feel I should answer her." I faced the woman that was trying so hard to embarrass me. "Mrs. Jessup, thank you for bringing this up to the group. I know that you're trying to demolish my reputation, perhaps cost me my marriage and destroy my position in the church, but this is a good time to tell you the facts. Yes, I was standing in the line with an application for Playboy, and that is me in the picture. However, the real reason is that I was pledging for a sorority and one of my big sisters didn't want to stand in that long line, so I had to stand for her. It was not my application. However, I am happy you brought this up tonight so we could clear this up."

Everyone looked in her direction waiting for a reply. She was so ashamed of trying to make me look bad that she apologized and left the room.

I accepted her apology and I said to the group, "It is things like this that makes a person not want to go to church. You see, we need to let our light shine. I have never done anything to her, and she needs to get over to the fact that I am married to the Pastor and accept Deborah's death."

Darlene said, "Ladies, I promise that nothing like this will ever happen again. We are to love one another and be a support for each other. If we look down at someone, it should only be to pick them up."

Mrs. Jessup came back into the room just in time for us to dismiss. We held hands, while Darlene asked us to repeat Proverbs 3:5-6 "Trust in the Lord with all thine heart and lean not unto thine own understanding. In all thy ways acknowledge him and he shall direct thy paths."

All of us hugged one another and called it a night. Mrs. Jessup hugged me and apologized again. She asked me not to tell Jonathan and I told her I wouldn't. All was forgiven and there was nothing more to say.

Chapter Eighteen

I rode home thinking about Mrs. Jessup and her attempt to discredit me. I was so happy she brought that up tonight. The devil meant if for evil but God turned it around for good. I hoped that her apology was sincere and that she would start treating me with respect. Now, I had to work on making John learn how to respect me.

I pulled into the garage tired and ready for bed, but when I walked into the house I found Jonathan cleaning up a mess on the kitchen floor.

"Jonathan, what happened in here?"

"David said he wasn't feeling too well. I told him to come in here and get a sprite and he vomited."

"Where is he?"

"Changing into another pair of pajamas."

"Why didn't you call me?"

"It just happened about 10 minutes ago."

"I'm going upstairs to see if it is anything I can do."

I knocked on David's door and heard a faint voice tell me to "come in." I walked in to find him laying in bed looking helpless. His cheeks were flushed, so I knew he had a fever. I also noticed red bumps on his arms and he was scratching them."

After greeting him and offering words of comfort, I returned downstairs to Jonathan.

"I think David has the chicken pox."

"Why do you think that?"

"Didn't you notice the red bumps on his arms?"

"No, I guess I was too busy cleaning up the vomit."

"I'm going to take his temperature. I need you to go to the drug store and get me some Tylenol for his fever and some calamine lotion."

While Jonathan went to the store, I took David's temperature. It was high.

Jonathan came back with the Tylenol and calamine lotion. I applied the lotion on David and gave him the proper medical dosage. Jonathan asked if I had chicken pox before. I told him yes. Luckily enough, so had he, but the other two boys had not. We told David that his brothers would need to stay away from him for a few days.

David wasn't happy. "You mean I have to stay in bed all weekend and miss camp?"

"Yes," I said gently. "You will be in this room for the next seven days. I plan to be here and take good care of you. I'll bring you your food..."

"Food? I don't feel like eating, I'm too tired, and my head hurts. I would like some cold ice tea though."

I went to get what he wanted. The other two boys were in the hall looking in at David. Dwayne wanted to know if he could catch what he had? I told him yes, that he and John had to stay out of David's room. Neither of the boys said anything. They just went back into their rooms.

After bringing David his tea, I sat in the chair and dozed off. Jonathan woke me up and took my place while I went to our room and caught some sleep. When I woke up and went upstairs. I found Jonathan asleep in the chair with his Bible in his lap. David was still sleeping.

I woke Jonathan and sent him off to his office to work on his sermon, and I told him that I would take care of David. I spent the night in his room applying lotion on his itching body and comforting him.

I woke up to the rays of the sun peeking through David's window blinds. I looked over and he was still asleep. When I went to wake Jonathan, he was already up and in the kitchen making breakfast. I told him to just feed the boys and after I freshened up, David and I would eat together.

I expected David to get better over the weekend, but his fever still wasn't down and he seemed to get worse. We put in an emergency call to his pediatrician who informed us that for some people it simply took a little longer for chicken pox to finish its course. Unfortunately, David was one of those people. By Sunday morning, he was still not feeling well. I stayed with him instead of going to church. While caring for David, I noticed the writing on the wall regarding going to Louisville on Monday.

While dialing Paula's cell number, I was thinking of the friction it would cause in this house if I went to Louisville tomorrow, while leaving a sick child behind. I didn't think that would go over well with Jonathan and it certainly would give John something else to throw up in my face as well as in his father's face. Paula answered on the third ring.

"Hello, Paula, this is Courtney. How are you?"

"I'm doing okay, just laying my clothes out for tomorrow and getting things ready for our trip."

"That's why I'm calling. My son, David, has chicken

pox and I don't feel right leaving him here with Jonathan. I plan to take time off until I'm sure that he is well."

"I don't blame you. I can take care of the business in Louisville. Don't worry. Everything will be okay."

"Thank you, Paula." I wanted to say I bet you will, but I just hung the telephone up.

I went back upstairs to check on David and he was fast asleep.

This gave me time to complete the dinner. Jonathan put the roast in the oven before leaving for church.

I heard the garage door go up and saw Jonathan and the boys pull inside. They were coming in from church. I was downstairs by the time they entered the house.

"How was church today?"

"Great!" Jonathan seemed energized. "Courtney, you missed it. I really felt good about the sermon. By the way, people were asking about you and David. I explained that you were home taking care of David. Even Mother Jessup asked about you."

"That was very nice of them. Now you three get out of those clothes and I'll get dinner on the table."

By the time the three of them came into the dinning room, I had set the table and brought out the Sunday dinner. It consisted of roast beef with carrots, potatoes and onions, steamed cabbage, macaroni and cheese, corn bread and sliced tomatoes. I even baked a chocolate cake with chocolate icing.

Jonathan's eyes lit up when he saw the table. "Now this is what I call a Sunday dinner fit for a king."

I grinned. "Well your majesty, you're my king."

My words pleased him, and during dinner his pleasured reached new heights when I told him that I wouldn't be going to Louisville, but staying home to take care of David. He tried talking me out of it, but I knew that he really felt good knowing that I had made the decision to stay home with our son.

Chapter Nineteen

After being home for a week taking care of David, it was more work than my day job. Cooking, cleaning and washing clothes. This is all that I did for the last four days. I was so happy Friday was here.

David is feeling better, and his bumps had healed. He was feeling so well that he asked Jonathan if he could go to the church with him, so his father took him. Meanwhile, John and Dwayne went to visit friends. I finally had the house to myself. This would be a good time to call Mary Ann to see how she and Martin are doing.

"Hello may I speak with MaryAnn Norwood."

"Hello, this is Mary Ann."

"Mary Ann, this is Courtney Davenport, you know the lady you met on Paradise Island."

"Yes, it is so good hearing from you. How have you been?"

"I'm still working full-time, but my youngest son came down with chicken pox, so I spent this week nursing him back to good health."

"I bet you have your hands full."

"You've got that right."

"When are you coming to visit our church?"

"I will have to talk this over with Jonathan because by him being the pastor, he usually limits his visits and stays home to deliver the sermon unless he is preaching at another church."

"Tell him, if he wants to rest one Sunday, please come and visit us."

"I will. If you and Martin are ever in the neighborhood, please come by for a visit. And, we must keep in touch."

"Yes we must. Just maybe one day we can meet for lunch."

"Sounds good to me, Mary Ann you take care."

It sure was good talking with her. I think I will call mom and dad and let them know that David is well now. They were calling all week wanting to come over and help. Morgan did her share of calling too. I'm so thankful for coming from such a loving and caring family.

After a hot bath, I relaxed with a good book when Jonathan and David came home with pizza, breadsticks and salad. I'm happy because I was in no mood for cooking. John and Dwayne came home shortly after, and Dwayne volunteered to set the table. John went upstairs. Ten minutes later, everyone was sitting at the table ready to eat, but John. I asked David to go get him.

Jonathan said "tomorrow is a good time to do our school shopping for the boys. Don't you think Courtney?"

"Jonathan since school is approaching yes I think we should get this task behind us."

John said "I sure hope you let me pick my own clothes. I'm fourteen and old enough to know what colors go together.

I wasn't going to war with John today, so I kept eating my pizza and let him and his father take on that discussion.

I'm learning how to fight the devil when he arrives in this house.

After dinner, Jonathan went into his study and I went into our room to call Paula to see how things went this week at work. Just as I picked up the receiver I heard shouting upstairs. I put the phone down and went running up there.

"What is going on up here?"

Angry tears were spilling down David's face. "Momma Courtney, I came in here and John was on his computer. I asked him if I could play a game. He started yelling at me to get out! And he said a bad word too."

By this time Jonathan was standing behind me.

"John, what did you say to your brother?" Jonathan demanded.

"I told him to get out of my room" John snapped defiantly.

"Did you say a cuss word? It was obvious that Jonathan wasn't going to tolerate that."

"No, David you're telling a big fat lie." He made a threatening move toward his brother, but Jonathan moved between them.

I addressed John. "Look here, young man, we don't use that kind of language around here. Do you hear me?"

Ignoring me, John turned around and started to hit the keys on his keyboard as if I wasn't talking to him. My anger started growing.

"John, I'm talking to you. Now get off that computer and listen to me!"

"Why should I? You're not my mother." John kept typing.

Jonathan started shouting. "John! You owe Courtney an apology, and I mean it right now!"

"I'm sorry." He didn't look at me and he wasn't sincere.

It was time for me to put him on the spot.

"I don't accept your apology, John. I'm not even sure who you are talking to?"

He was defiant. "I'm talking to you."

"John!" Jonathan reacted to his tone.

"If you are talking to me, then what's my name?"

His eyes narrowed as he turned and looked me in the face. "Your name is Ms. Courtney Davis."

I was stunned and I was hurt. Without a word, I turned and left the room. I could hear Jonathan yelling at him, as I headed down the stairs, grabbed my purse and keys, went to the garage and got into my car. I wasn't sure where I was going, but I had to get away from here.

I ended up at Morgan's house. When she opened the door, I gave her a big hug and burst into tears. She was surprised.

"Courtney, why the tears?"

She moved me into the house and my frustrations and disappointment poured from me. I told her about how John keeps something going on in the house all the time, and I have so much on my plate. I work full-time. I spend a lot of time at the church. I have to take care of home and it's all too much!

Morgan listened to me, comforted me and prayed with me. I thanked God for her. Finally, it was time for me to go home and face the music.

When I arrived the house was dark. It was late; I

figured that Jonathan and the boys were asleep. I was wrong. He was waiting up for me.

"Are you okay?" He looked worried and concerned.

Too drained to do more, I nodded in the affirmative, and went down the hall to our bedroom. As I started to undress, I heard a faint knock on the door.

"Who is it?"

"It's me Momma Courtney, Dwayne."

"Come on in hun. What can I do for you?"

"I just want you to know that I love you and I don't want you to leave us."

I looked at him in surprise. "Dwayne, what are you talking about? I just went to my sister's house to spend a little time with her. I'm not leaving you."

"I heard Dad getting on John about his mouth and not respecting you, then you left upset. I just want us to be a family."

I hugged him. "Dwayne, I love you and your brothers. We are a family." Just as we were hugging David came into the room and hugged me too.

"I love you Momma Courtney."

"I love you too David. Now, you both go to bed and get your rest."

Dwayne closed the door behind him, but it opened again. This time it was Jonathan standing in the doorway.

"So Momma Courtney, you have spies in the camp."

"I guess so. I'm glad they love me and want me to stay."

"They aren't the only one. I love you too Mrs. Davenport."

Chapter Twenty

Good morning Holy Spirit, the sun is bright and I made up my mind that I wasn't going to let anything happen to me today, that the Lord and I couldn't handle. I looked over and Jonathan wasn't in the room. I looked at the clock and it was a little after ten. I put on my robe and rushed to the family room to see why Jonathan allowed me to sleep so late. The house was quiet. I started calling out the boys names and there was no answer. I went to look in Jonathan's office and he wasn't there. I called his cell to see where they were. Jonathan said he and the boys were shopping and for me to take the day for myself.

I spent most of the day relaxing, reading, and making calls to family and friends. Just as I was coming from our room I heard the garage open. I went into the family room to welcome them back. David and Dwayne were so excited about their new clothes. They asked if I would come up and see them. John rushed pass me with his bags. He didn't say anything and neither did I.

While upstairs looking at Dwayne and David's new outfits, Jonathan yelled for us to come and eat. He had brought sub sandwiches for lunch. When I got in the kitchen, he was holding a vase full of beautiful red roses and smiling.

"Oh Jonathan, these are beautiful. Thank you."

"After shopping, the boys and I went to the florist and got these for you. You have been so busy taking care of David and now about to return to work Monday for the first time in a week. I just wanted to show you how much you are appreciated around here."

"Jonathan when the boys come to the table I must thank them. These are beautiful."

After lunch John went to his room, while Dwayne and David went bike riding. Jonathan went to his office, while I went into our room to do a little Bible reading.

Later, Jonathan entered the room. He was dressed in his nice navy suit. I was about to say something, when he said, "The boys will not be coming home tonight. I'm taking them to my parents, so we can go out."

"Jonathan, that sounds good."

"Where are you taking me?"

"It's a surprise, so just get dressed"

I got dress in my designer navy sparkling dress with a v shape in the back. I had on my navy shoes with matching handbag. He kept complimenting me on the dress.

We rode downtown in silence. When he pulled up in the front of my favorite downtown restaurant, I smiled.

The valet parked the car. We were seated at one of the best tables and were treated like royalty. The conversation was nice and the food was delicious. I was starting to enjoy myself.

After dinner, Jonathan asked, "Do you have room for desserts?"

"Why yes, I always have room for desserts."

Instead of ordering it in the restaurant, we got back in the car and drove up the street to the Hilton hotel. I wanted to ask him why we would leave one restaurant and go to another for desserts, but I didn't. I just went along for the ride.

We entered the hotel and walked pass the restaurant to

the waiting elevators and Jonathan pushed the button to the 11th floor. I didn't say a word I simply followed him to the room.

When he opened the door, there on a sterling silver tray with an assortment of desserts. Fresh rose petals were scattered on the floor leading to the bedroom. I just looked around the room in amazement.

Jonathan grinned. "Well, Mrs. Davenport, this is where we will be spending the night. I knew how hard it has been taking care of our sick son, and I wanted to show you how much you are loved and appreciated."

All I could say was, "Oh Jonathan, just hold me."

Chapter Twenty One

Good morning Holy Spirit, today is Monday and what a glorious day! I'm sill floating on clouds about what happened to me this weekend after a difficult week with David's illness.

As I pulled into the parking lot, I still felt great. When I walked into the office, I found Julia at her desk just as cheerful as ever. Mr. East's office was dark and Paula was in her office on the telephone, so I waved at her and went to my office.

Later, Paula came into my office and wanted to know how things were going in my house. I told her and she told me about the trip to Louisville. From the sound of it, it went very well. We talked for about ten minutes and she left my office.

Julia came into my office. She started telling me about a conversation she over heard between Paula and Mr. East. I stopped her.

"I do not want to hear any gossip. If there is something I need to know, I'll wait for the memo."

She just shook her head, left my office and didn't say another word. I was in no mood for gossip. I had too much catching up to do.

I closed my door to continue to open my snail mail, emails and to make some appointments for the rest of the week. I looked up, and it was time for lunch. I really wasn't too hungry, as I was heading towards the vending machines, my telephone rang and it was my mother. Dad was complaining about having a terrible headache. She and Morgan were taking him to see his doctor. She told me not to worry, that if it was serious, she would call me.

I tried to work, but my mind was on my father. I wanted to know what was happening with him. I called Jonathan and asked him to please remember my dad in prayer. I continued to work when another call came through. It was mom. She and Morgan were on the way to the emergency room. My father's condition was worsening. I told her I'd meet them there.

When I got to St. Vincent Hospital and asked for my father. The nurse told me to come with her. I followed her to a room where Mom and Morgan were sitting. They were crying. There was a Chaplain in the room with them. I froze. Mom looked at me and said the words that I feared most. "Dad is gone."

I couldn't comprehend what she was saying. "Dad is gone? But, he only had a headache."

Morgan sobbed. "The doctor said he was hemorrhaging from a brain tumor that burst."

I couldn't believe it. My father was dead. The three of us clung to each other crying. I called Jonathan to let him know that my father had died.

I spent the next four days at my mother's side helping to make arrangements. Mom was a wreck and really couldn't do anything. Morgan and I handled it all. Jonathan was my anchor. It was his suggestion that I stay with my mom until after the funeral.

The day after my father's service, I returned home. I was exhausted physically, mentally and spiritually. Jonathan met me at the door and I rushed to his waiting arms. I couldn't help but to cry. As he held me he told me, "You can make it. God won't put anymore on you than you are able to handle." Little did I know that when I returned to work the next week my trials would not be over.

When I got to work that morning, Julia wasn't at her desk. I made a mental note to thank her for the flowers and a card she had sent to our family. I went straight to my office. I wasn't in there long before Paula came in and shut the door behind her.

"Courtney I'm sorry about your father's death, but we need to talk."

I didn't like her attitude or her approach, but I caught myself and remained professional.

"What do we need to talk about, Paula?"

"Your work ethic. You've taken entirely too many days off from work."

I swallowed and took a deep breath. She was going too far.

"When did you become my boss?"

She looked me straight into my eyes and said "On Friday."

I was stunned. "On Friday? What are you talking about?"

"Since I'm doing all the work, Mr. East promoted me last Friday. I don't mean to be rude, but we have a lot of work to do and it looks like you can't handle it." With those words, she left my office.

I was furious. I locked my door, and through silent tears I typed my letter of resignation. I went to her office, placed it on her desk and stood there.

She seemed surprised as she read it, and had the nerve to ask me why I was doing this.

I told her, "Don't you think for one moment that I have not been aware of your all of your lies and schemes. I am no fool. I know that from day one your intentions were to have my job! Don't you sit here and put it on my work ethic since it is so bad then you have two weeks to find someone to do my job."

She was so upset with me that she shouted, "I don't need two weeks, you can pack your things and leave now! By the way, you are exactly right. I wanted your job and look, now I have it."

I did as she said, packed my belongings and walked right past Mr. East's still darkened office. When I got to the door Julia was coming in. She asked me why was I carrying a box of my personal belongings?

I told her, "Ask boss Paula. She is the one who fired me."

Julia didn't seem too surprised. "I tried to warn you."

She was right. She had.

Chapter Twenty Two

Today is the first day of school. I crawled out of bed in plenty of time to make sure that the boys had a wholesome breakfast before going to school. Dwayne was the first to enter the kitchen. That boy loves to eat. I had the food waiting for him. I prepared link and pan sausage, scrabbled eggs, grits, biscuits, orange juice and milk. I wanted to make pancakes, but I didn't want the sugar to make them hyper on the first day of school.

By the time all three of the boys were down for breakfast, Jonathan was in the family room reading the morning paper. When he heard me say breakfast was ready, he came in to inspect how they were dressed for school. They had on their collared shirts, belts in the loop of their pants and nice white tennis shoes. I found myself feeling pretty proud of them. After breakfast, we formed a circle. Jonathan led us in a word of prayer. He didn't want our children to leave the house without being covered by the blood of Jesus.

After the last bus pulled up and John was safely on it. I went back into the kitchen to clean up the breakfast dishes. I put my thick rump roast in the crock pot with onions, potatoes and carrots on low for dinner. Jonathan said he was going to church a little early, which was okay with me. I had plans to go shopping just as soon as the store doors opened. My plans were for Jonathan and the boys to come home and notice the new curtains in the kitchen.

Around ten o'clock I got my purse and was ready to go shopping. The phone started ringing almost off the hook. It was Mary Ann she wanted us to meet for lunch around noon. I told her I was on my way shopping in the Castleton area, so we made plans to meet at a restaurant there.

After shopping and having lunch with Mary Ann, I made it home just before Jonathan. He rushed in with a big smile on his face. He was so excited he couldn't get the words out. He was invited to attend a conference in Chicago. I was happy for him. This would give me some quality time with the boys.

I went into the kitchen to finish dinner. Jonathan came in and immediately noticed the new curtains, plants, and decorations. He admired how colorful the kitchen looked. I thanked him for his compliments.

We heard the bus arrive, when David was the first to walk in. He had so much to say about his first day. He labeled it as a fun day. Dwayne came in with a frown on his face. He was upset about all the homework his teachers gave him. I told him that our daily schedule would consist of changing your school clothes, eating dinner and sitting at the kitchen table to do homework. John came in just as I was giving the instructions. He looked at me like I was crazy. He said "why can't I do my homework in my room?" I told him that was not a problem. I will be checking all of their homework when it is completed.

For the next couple of days I cleaned the house a little, did some of the laundry and napped before the boys came in from school. Thursday morning Jonathan was packed and ready for the airport. He called the boys into the family room, to tell them about his trip. He told them to respect the rules of the house, and to be kind to me. He hugged them and ended our little meeting with prayer.

They agreed to follow the rules then they rushed back upstairs to get dressed for school. Jonathan didn't want any breakfast, so he had a cup of coffee. I walked him to the waiting taxi cab. He promised to call me when he arrived and let me hear from him once a day. He kissed me and said his goodbye.

The boys were gone to school when the phone started to ring. It was Jonathan. He wanted me to know that his plane had arrived safely in Chicago. He was on his way to the hotel for check in. I told him the boys got off to school and I was cleaning the kitchen.

After dinner the boys started on their homework and I went into the bedroom to call Morgan. I wanted to make an appointment to meet her at the bridal shop tomorrow to see the dresses. I called her and got no answer. I tried her on her cell and it went straight to voice mail. I thought that was odd, but then maybe she and Christopher were out with friends and just did not want to be interrupted. I found myself getting a little sleepy so I just laid there and went to sleep.

"Momma Courtney! Momma Courtney! Are you asleep?"

"It was David Oh, thank you for waking me. I'm supposed to look over your brother's homework."

"Dwayne left his homework on the kitchen table for you to look at, but John is in his room on his computer. He won't let me play one game."

"David, thank you I'll handle this."

I washed the sleep out my eye and went upstairs to see what John was up too. I stood outside the door and knocked before entering.

"John, can I come in?"

"Just a minute I..I..I'm putting on my pajamas."

"Take your time. I just want to look over your homework."

"I haven't finished it yet. You don't need to worry about checking it. It isn't due until next Wednesday. I'll have it done before then. I promise to let you read over my essay when I'm finished."

"Okay, then you finish getting dressed and don't forget to wash your face and brush your teeth before turning in."

"I won't."

I must be crazy talking to him through a closed and possible locked door. I think when he leaves for school tomorrow I'm going to look at that computer to see what he is up too.

Chapter Twenty Three

Today is Friday, thank God for Friday. I smiled as I was making my bed. I missed Jonathan, but it was easier to make a bed in which only one person has slept. I rushed in the kitchen to make pancakes, bacon and pan sausages for breakfast. The boys have been good since their father has been away, so they deserved a treat. I put a bowl of freshly cut fruit on the table. Dwayne entered the kitchen.

"Good morning Momma Courtney, you sure do have this kitchen smelling good."

"Dwayne, you sure do know how to make me feel good."

"I'll go upstairs and get David and John if you want me too."

"Yes, please, so their pancakes will be nice and hot."

He went through the house yelling. "We got pancakes this morning. You better come to the table."

After breakfast, Dwayne and David went outside to wait for their bus, but John went back upstairs. I thought he was getting his books, but he stayed a little too long. I went upstairs and he was on his computer. I cleared my throat and he jumped, turned the computer off and rushed pass me and down the stairs to catch his bus.

I followed him downstairs and watched from the window as he boarded the bus. I was about to go upstairs to see what was keeping him on that computer so much, but I was feeling a little dizzy. I sat on the bottom step until the feeling passed, then I got up and slowly walked to our bedroom to lie down until I felt a little better.

After a short rest, I decided to call Morgan. I've been trying to get in touch with her since yesterday, but again I got no answer. I tried her cell and again, it went into voice mail. Just as I hung up the telephone rang.

"Hello."

"Courtney, by now the boys are gone what are you doing?"

"Jonathan, how are you? I'm resting. I was on my way upstairs when a sick spell came over me, but I feel better now."

"Do you think you should call a doctor?"

"No, I'll be okay."

"Is John acting up?"

"Surprisingly, no, his computer is keeping him company."

"Well, things are going very well here in Chicago. I do miss you and the boys. Today, I will be meeting with three other Pastors. I will have so much to share with you when I get home."

"You just take care of yourself and we will be waiting to see you Sunday. I will tell the boys you said hello and send your love."

"Take care and remember I love you."

"I love you too Jonathan."

I thought about what Jonathan said about me seeing a doctor, but before I do that I think I will go to the drug store and buy a pregnancy kit. My body doesn't feel normal and I am tired and just want to sleep.

I got dressed and went grocery shopping. As I walked down the aisle, I wandered into the pharmacy department and bought the most expensive pregnancy kit they had. If I was pregnant I wanted it to be accurate.

When I arrived home there were two messages on my answering machine from Morgan. She sounded so excited and kept saying for me to call her when I got the message. I called her.

"Morgan, I have been trying to call you, but you haven't been answering your phone. Where are you?"

"Courtney, are you sitting down?"

"Yes."

"Christopher and I are in Las Vegas and we got married this morning!"

I almost dropped the telephone. "Morgan I think we have a bad connection. Did I hear you say that you and Christopher got married today?"

"You got it. Since Dad's death I've been wondering who would walk me down the aisle. Christopher has been on my case about us just flying to Vegas and getting married, so I took him up on it. This way it didn't cost much and we can have a wedding reception at a later date."

"Morgan did you tell Mom?"

"Not yet, we will tell her in person when we get back Sunday. We are having so much fun. Sis please, please be happy for me."

"I'm just sad that I wasn't there to witness such a beautiful occasion."

"I told you we'll still have a wedding reception. I better go. Christopher rented a car and we're going to tour Vegas. I love you and see you Sunday."

When I hung up the phone I said to myself "Now I do feel like I'm going to faint." I couldn't believe it. Morgan was married. Wow!!

Chapter Twenty Four

Today was Saturday, Jonathan would be home from the conference tomorrow, and I thought that this was a good time to use the pregnancy kit and see if I was pregnant. If so, I could tell Jonathan the good news tomorrow. If not, then I would keep it to myself.

Just as I was waiting for the results, Jonathan called. He wanted to know how things were going with the boys. I told him that, amazingly, even John was treating me nice. He was happy to know that things were going well and reminded me that he will be home tomorrow afternoon. I told him that I couldn't wait to see him.

I went back into the bathroom to check if the results were positive or negative. I almost screamed. It was positive! Oh my God! Jonathan and I are going to have a baby! Now to keep this a secret until he gets home will be the hard part.

I hid my excitement as I rounded the boys up to take them to the Church's Youth Day. I had to prod John off of his computer by demanding that he get off of it right now and come on. I surprised him and he nearly jumped off the chair and ran pass me down the stairs.

I dropped the boys off at the church and accepted Darlene's offer to bring them back home after they helped her clean up. I hurried back home. I couldn't wait to get on

John's computer to see what was taking up all his time.

I went to his room, Lucky for me, his computer was still on. He had minimized his email. I opened it and read all the conversations he was having with a young girl who said that she was fifteen. As I read, I couldn't believe the language that was on those emails. I kept thinking that this conversation sure didn't sound like a fifteen-year-old. The more I read the more upset I was getting, especially at the last entry. The two of them had made plans to meet in the back parking lot of Lafayette Square Mall at five o'clock today. John was scheduled to be at the Youth Day until six o'clock. How was he supposed to meet this girl at the mall?

I looked at the clock on the computer. It was four o'clock. I called the church to speak with Darlene to see if the boys were still with her. I didn't get an answer. I called her cell. She answered with a pleasant "hello."

I asked if she had the boys with her. She said yes, all but John.

"He grabbed a ride with one of the older boys who were going to the mall for a while. He called you and got your permission to go. I heard him talk to you on a cell phone."

I told her I didn't know anything about this, but if she would take Dwayne and David to her house I'd pick them up later. She heard the fear in my voice and asked if everything was all right. I told her yes, I would talk to her later.

What to do? What to do? My God, Jonathan was out-of-town. I didn't know what to do. But, as always, God was there right-on-time. The telephone rang. It was Mary Ann Norwood.

I remembered that her husband is a police officer in

the West District of Indianapolis. She was calling to ask if Jonathan and I would like to join them for dinner this evening.

Mary Ann must have heard the distress in my voice because she asked if I was okay. After telling her everything, Mary Ann insisted that she and her husband help me to find John.

I ran to the car and drove at a speed that felt like ninety miles an hour to the mall. The Norwoods met me at the mall entrance.

"Martin, Mary Ann, thank you for meeting me here." I was never happier to see any two people in my life.

I led them through the mall where John's email said that he and the girl would be meeting.

We had just exited one of the stores leading to the parking lot where the rendezvous was to take place, when I saw John talking to some man. I alerted the Norwoods,

"There's John, the boy in the blue shirt and jeans, the one standing there with that man."

Martin stepped forward. "Courtney, you stay here. John doesn't know me, so he might think I'm just a shopper. I'll go talk to him."

The words had hardly left my lips when suddenly the man grabbed John. He and the man struggled as an attempt was made to drag him toward a white van. I screamed. Whipping out his cell phone, Martin started walking and talking as he hurried toward them. I was right behind him and Mary Ann was on my heels. I watched as the man practically dragged John across the parking lot, but he resisted. I yelled out John's name as the three of us got closer to them.

Just as the stranger threw John into the van and closed the door, Martin rushed him and wrestled him to the ground. As they wrestled on the ground, John leaped from the van. He saw me and ran to my waiting arms. He was hysterical.

"Momma Courtney, that man tried to kidnap me!"

I kept telling him that he was safe with me. Meanwhile, the police arrived a few seconds later. The rest was a blur as a crowd gathered and the authorities questioned us. They mentioned finding a roll of duck tape, a rope and a syringe filled with clear liquids in the van.

I fell on my knees right in the parking lot and thanked God for sparing John's life. John was crying and so was I.

As the media began to gather, John and I were given permission by the authority to leave. Neither of us was prepared to face a media circus. Both of us were shaken by the reality of what could have happened to him, so Mary Ann offered to drive our car, while Martin follow in theirs. There was no way I could have thanked them enough for what they had done for us. They were both miracles sent by God.

When we arrived at the house, the answering machine was filled to capacity. Obviously, word had spread about the attempted abduction. However, I didn't want to talk to anyone until I spoke to Jonathan first. I tried his cell, but it went straight to voice mail. I left an urgent message for him to call me, both on his cell and at the hotel desk.

I called Darlene to let her know that I was home with John. When she arrived with Dwayne and David, I explained to them what happened. Upset, the boys rushed upstairs to

John's room to see about him.

Just as I was about to go upstairs to make sure the boys were okay, the phone started ringing. It was Jonathan.

"What's going on?"

"Jonathan, don't get upset until you hear me out. John was on his computer talking with who he thought was a fifteen-year-old girl. He made plans to meet her at the mall, but it turned out to be a thirty-year-old man. He tried to kidnap him."

I proceeded to tell him about the Martin's remarkable rescue, and the miracle that sent the Norwoods to me at the right time.

"Thank you, God", was all he could say. I second that.

Despite my protest, Jonathan took the first flight out of Chicago to Indianapolis. When the boys and I picked him up at the airport, the boys and I clung to him for dear life, including John.

Sunday morning, was indeed a beautiful day. When Jonathan, me and the boys arrived at church, the congregation showed us plenty of love. I asked Jonathan last night if I could have a few minutes to speak to the congregation after Darlene gives the announcements. He gave me the okay.

After Darlene made the weekly announcements, I stood and walked to the microphone. I thanked everyone for their prayers and good wishes for our family. I told them how important it was for parents to monitor their children on the computer in the home. I said that they need to make sure that their children are using it for homework and not chatting in those chat rooms. Just as I finished and was about to walk to my seat, to my surprise John came up to the podium.

He said, "Momma Courtney, I would like to thank you for caring for me enough to look at my computer. I also want to let you know that I am so sorry for how I have treated you. If it wasn't for you and the good Lord, I might not be here today."

I looked at him. Tears were streaming down his face.

"John, I accept your apology, and I want you to know that I love you."

As we took our seats, the entire congregation was on its feet clapping. My heart was full.

That evening, the entire family had dinner at our house. Morgan and Christopher had returned from their honeymoon. Mom was back from visiting her sister and Jonathan's parents were in attendance as well. We talked about what had happened to John and then I stood to make an announcement.

"I would like to say that I love each of you sitting in this room. I am also happy to announce that Jonathan and I are having a baby."

John got up and hugged me. "I sure hope it's a girl. That's the only thing that's missing in this family."

Everyone looked at him in amazement. Then Morgan stood and said something even more amazing.

"Since we all are giving out good news today, stand up Christopher, we must tell ours." Her new husband stood beside her and she continued. "We are expecting a little one too." Everyone burst into applause.

Finally, Mom stood and said "I'm not standing because I'm pregnant, but because I'm feeling good and sad at the same time. I'm feeling good that the family is growing and sad because your father isn't here to share this great experience. But, I've got to say that when the time comes for babysitting, I'll just have to ask God to give me strength for the journey."

About The Author

Francine A. Yates lives in Indianapolis, Indiana with her husband Benjamin and her two children Donald and Patrice. She attended Indiana University/Purdue University in Indianapolis.

Fran has been a mentor at an Indianapolis public school. She created a book club at the Wheelers Boys & Girls Club of Indianapolis.

Fran's active membership includes: Pleasant Union Missionary Baptist Church, Church Women United, and Authors Supporting Authors Positively (ASAP).

Fran's work has been published in the *Indianapolis Star*, and in 2003 she founded Yates Publishing, LLC.

To schedule Book Signings or Speaking Engagements Contact:

> Francine A. Yates
> P.O. Box 18982
> Indianapolis, IN 46218
> Fran3214@yahoo.com
> www.franyates.net

www.ingramcontent.com/pod-product-compliance
Lightning Source LLC
Chambersburg PA
CBHW072000170626
46813CB00005B/1952